The Savage Gorge is, sadly, Colin Forbes' last novel. He delivered the completed manuscript to his publishers at the end of July and three weeks later, on 23rd August 2006, he died. Simon & Schuster are honoured to publish *The Savage Gorge* in memory of Colin and his long, distinguished career as the author of 33 internationally bestselling thrillers.

THE
SAVAGE
GORGE

COLIN FORBES

POCKET
BOOKS

LONDON • SYDNEY • NEW YORK • TORONTO

First published in Great Britain by Simon & Schuster UK Ltd, 2006
This edition first published by Pocket Books, 2007
An imprint of Simon & Schuster UK Ltd
A CBS COMPANY

1 3 5 7 9 10 8 6 4 2

Simon & Schuster UK Ltd
Africa House
64–78 Kingsway
London WC2B 6AH

www.simonsays.co.uk

Simon & Schuster Australia
Sydney

A CIP catalogue record for this book is available
from the British Library

ISBN-13: 978-1-4165-2643-8
EAN-10: 1-4165-2643-9

Typeset in Plantin by M Rules
Printed and bound in Great Britain by
Cox & Wyman Ltd, Reading, Berks

Author's Note

All characters are inventions and do not exist in real life. Equally, all towns, villages, counties, shops, residences and companies are inventions on the part of the author of this novel.

THE
SAVAGE
GORGE

Prologue

It started with the terrified scream of a frightened girl.

Tweed, ace detective at the Yard before he accepted the post of Deputy Chief of the SIS, frowned as he sat behind his desk in his spacious first-floor office. He had just finished reading his instructions to an agent in Europe. The scream had broken his concentration.

'London gets rowdier day by day,' he grumbled.

The only two other occupants of the room were Monica, absorbed by her typing at her desk behind the closed door, and Tweed's second-in-command, Paula Grey, who had stood up from her desk to peer down through an open window into Park Crescent. It was a glorious May day. The sun shone out of a duck-egg-blue sky.

Paula, in her thirties, had thick glossy hair falling

almost to her shoulders. Her features were well-shaped: a high forehead, neat eyebrows above alert blue-grey eyes, a strong nose with a firm mouth and determined chin.

The girl who had screamed was hurrying towards their entrance. Frequently she glanced back over her shoulder. No one else about. It was that brief period when commuters had arrived at work and the shoppers were not yet out and about.

'I think she's coming here,' Paula reported.

'Who is?' growled Tweed.

'The girl who screamed.'

'Well, we can do without her.'

The phone rang. Monica, in late middle-age, hair tied in a bun, Tweed's loyal secretary for many years, also acted as switchboard operator. She picked up the phone, listened, stared at Tweed.

'George,' she said, referring to the ex-army guard in the hall, 'says a Miss Lisa Clancy needs to see you urgently . . .'

'Well,' Tweed said decisively, 'I don't want to see her. So get George to send her on her way.'

Monica, looking puzzled, resumed her conversation, which seemed to stretch out. Paula walked across to her. With a thankful expression Monica handed her the phone. Paula's conversation was brief. Cupping her hand over the phone, she stared at Tweed.

'You *will* see her. She was recommended to contact you by her friend Crystal Main, chief accountant of the Main Chance Bank.'

2

'Then I haven't much choice, have I? Wheel her up.'

Swiftly he packed the ten red folders answering queries from ten agents in Europe into a large metal box, locked it, put his key in a bottom drawer, which he also locked. He called across to Monica.

'Since the rest of our team is out checking different areas in London, call Communications to send two guards to collect this.' Communications was in a separate house further along the Crescent; its sophisticated aerials were disguised as TV masts. 'When they arrive,' Tweed added, 'tell them everything is for immediate transmission after coding.'

Paula returned to her distant corner desk, where she could get a good view of the unwanted visitor. She checked on Tweed. She saw a well-built man of medium height, middle-aged but these days he was looking younger. He had neatly brushed thick dark hair, an unlined forehead, large blue eyes which missed nothing, a long nose above a wide strong mouth and a firm jaw. He could change his expression from aggression to amiability in a split second. Despite his earlier mood he now looked relaxed.

The door opened after a discreet tap. George ushered in an attractive blonde in her late thirties. Expensively dressed, she wore a short white pleated skirt, a stylish leather jacket, a tasteful cravat round her long neck.

'Miss Lisa Clancy.' George introduced her and withdrew.

'Welcome.' Tweed stood up. The visitor hastily

3

removed a silk glove to grasp his outstretched hand gently. 'Do sit down,' Tweed urged, indicating the carver chair in front of his desk. 'May I ask your name?' he enquired, settling back in his chair. George had only mumbled it.

'I am . . . Lisa . . . Clancy. Miss.'

She kept swallowing. Although she had a soft pleasant voice, she appeared to have difficulty in speaking. She crossed her legs, then recrossed them. Her small shapely hands kept twisting her glove. Her large blue eyes flickered round the office.

A bundle of nerves, thought Paula, who was studying her discreetly.

Monica stood up, went to her side, smiling. 'Would you like a cup of coffee?'

Thank you. If . . . it's not . . . too much bother.'

'No bother at all,' Monica assured her cheerfully. 'Milk? Do you take sugar?'

'Just black . . . It is . . . so kind of you.'

'Back in a minute,' Monica said with another smile and left the room.

Miss Clancy began to tremble. She clasped both hands tightly over the glove. Her shoulders began shaking. Pursing her lips tightly, she sat up very straight, pressed her back against the chair, uncrossed her legs and sat with her knees close together. An atmosphere of fear began to emanate from their visitor.

Paula was waiting for Tweed to cut the interview short, to get her out of the building. Women all over London were complaining of being stalked. A minority

4

were disappointed when no man took any notice of them. Now the sensation of fear percolating through their office changed Tweed's approach.

'I need a few facts,' he suggested pleasantly. 'Were you stalked when you came here?'

'Yes, I was.'

No, you weren't, Paula said to herself, I'd have seen anyone when I watched you coming round the Crescent, but she changed her mind as Lisa Clancy explained.

'He – or she – disappeared into the shrubbery on the other side of the main road. They were watching me through binoculars – I saw the sunlight flashing off the lenses. I think they checked your name plate on the wall to see where I was going. The General and Cumbria Assurance Company.'

She had quoted the cover name for the SIS. Typically, her friend Crystal Main had omitted to mention the SIS.

'He or she? They?' Tweed said immediately. 'Do you mean there are two of them stalking you? One man, one woman?'

Lisa was thanking Monica, who had arrived with a steaming cup of black coffee. She took a sip, then replied, 'Sometimes it's a hunchback with long greasy hair carrying a big executive case. Then he disappears into an alley. A few minutes later it's a woman wearing a long black dress with a veil covering her face.'

'I see,' said Tweed, who didn't. 'How long has this been going on?'

'Five days. This is the fifth day.'

'Have you any enemies? Say a boyfriend you've dropped and who's furious with you?'

In the last few moments, Paula noticed Lisa appeared to have gained control over herself, was speaking normally without choking out the words. That changed.

'Do you live and work in London?' Tweed asked her suddenly.

'Yes. I'm training to be . . . an accountant . . . with Rumble, Crowther and Nicholas. Their offices . . . are only a short . . . walk from where I'm renting a nice house. I'm . . . quite well . . . off. In a street leading off Bexford Street . . . a side street with another . . . side street. I feel so guilty.'

'Guilty? About what?'

'Taking up . . . so much of your time. Could you escort me home? I couldn't stand . . . being . . . stalked again. I know I shouldn't ask you to do this for me.'

'Yes, of course we'll see you safely back. Ready now?'

It was her emphasis on the word 'guilty' which alerted Tweed, as it had Paula. Guilty of what? The reason Lisa had given was not convincing. Paula checked her Browning .32 automatic which was tucked inside a holster strapped to her lower left leg and was escorting Lisa down the stairs with Tweed behind her when Harry Butler, the toughest and cleverest member of Tweed's team, came into the office. Tweed called down to the two women.

'Wait in the hall for me. Only be a moment.'

He followed Harry into his office, closed the door carefully, gave him his instructions. He described the strange characters Lisa had alleged had stalked her, told Harry to collect his car from the park at the back of the building.

'Sounds crazy,' Harry agreed, 'but I'll be not far behind your Audi. You won't see me.'

'The target never does when you are following him . . .'

When Paula opened a rear door of the Audi she expected Lisa to sit on the pavement side. But no, she dived across and chose the seat overlooking the street. Paula sat beside her as Tweed took the wheel. Bexford Street? It was curious that Lisa lived in a rented house quite close to the stately terraced house he had purchased just before the property boom.

'It's the next side street,' Lisa called out as they passed Tweed's home. They turned, drove down a narrower deserted side street. 'Then,' she continued, 'you turn left and my place is the first on the left round the corner.'

Guilty? The word kept reverberating through Tweed's head. He was totally unprepared for the ghastly shock awaiting him.

1

Police tape was strung across the entrance to the house on the corner, before Tweed turned into the next quiet street, the house next to Lisa's round the corner. He was driving slowly, pulled in next to the tape. As he alighted, telling his passengers to wait in the car, Paula glanced at Lisa. She was staring fixedly at the street on her side.

Tweed crouched down by the body spread out down the steps. It had been covered with a bedsheet but no policeman was on guard. Slipping on latex gloves, he lifted the sheet at the top, sucked in his breath.

Not a pleasant sight. It was the body of a well-dressed woman in her late thirties or early forties. He lifted an arm. Rigor mortis had come and gone – which meant she had been lying there for hours. Probably murdered during the night.

Her slender throat had been slashed open from ear to ear. Tweed felt real horror seeing what had once been a handsome face. Past tense. Her forehead, cheeks, nose and chin had been gutted with some strange instrument; a series of deep squiggles had rendered her, he felt sure, unrecognizable. Such brutal butchery he had not experienced before.

'I've never seen anything as hideous as this,' Paula's calm voice said over his shoulder. 'Don't worry – I've left Lisa in the car, locked all the doors.'

He replaced the sheet over the horrific face, walked down the steps, continued round the corner to Lisa's house. No police tape there. But the house beyond did have more police tape – and another body sprawled down the steps, also covered with a sheet. No police guard.

Climbing the steps, still wearing the latex gloves, he lifted the sheet. Like the previous corpse it was a woman, of a similar age, with fairish hair and was expensively dressed. Her face had been ruined with a similar weird instrument – or the same one. Deep squiggles of flesh had been torn open, were coated with dried blood. Her throat was slashed from ear to ear. Tweed lifted an arm. No rigor mortis. This body had also lain here for hours.

The door to the house was jerked open, slammed back. A figure stood in the doorway in a police uniform. It was a tall overweight officer, his peaked cap on his head above cunning eyes glaring viciously at Tweed. Chief Inspector Reedbeck.

'Heavens!' whispered Paula. 'Old Roadblock.' Her nickname for the most incompetent police officer Tweed had ever met.

'What are you doing messing about here?' the officer demanded snidely. 'Commander Buchanan has placed me in sole charge of this murder investigation. And already I have the killer locked up in our new Pine Street police station just down the road.'

'Chief Inspector Roadblock—' Tweed started again: Paula had thumped him in the ribs. 'Chief Inspector Reedbeck,' he began grimly, 'how long have the two bodies been lying on their doorsteps? And surely you're not alone?'

'Of course not,' Reedbeck snapped. 'I have Sergeant Peabody and Constable Brown with me.'

'Then why aren't they here guarding the bodies? And how long have you been here? Why hasn't the pathologist arrived?'

'Because –' Reedbeck had folded his arms, his expression distinctly smug – 'Peabody and Brown are inside the houses trying to establish the victims' identities. Nothing in their handbags . . .'

'Both men should be outside guarding the bodies. You could deal with searching the houses.'

'I don't need any lessons from you, Tweed. And I've been here two hours. I'm waiting for the pathologist I phoned almost that long ago, Professor Arpfels.'

'Why not Professor Saafeld? He'd have been here ages ago and the bodies would be in his mortuary.'

'Your pet pathologist,' Reedbeck sneered.

11

'Who happens to be the top pathologist in the country. Arpfels is useless. And what is this about your having a serial killer at Pine Street? What is his name – and what evidence have you to charge him with this beastly crime?'

'Well, even you know that. A murderer often returns to the scene of his crime. I spotted this joker stopping, looking at the body here, then going round the corner and stopping again to stare at the other corpse. I dashed out and nabbed him.'

'He went under the police tapes and examined the faces?'

'Well, no he didn't.' Reedbeck was losing some of his arrogant self-confidence. 'He refused to give his name, refused to say one word to me or at the police station. I had him searched, but he'd nothing on him to say who he was. Don't you find that significant?'

'Maybe you didn't search him thoroughly.' Tweed raised his voice. 'I think you're disgraceful – leaving two corpses out in the open without guards. The Yard could well do without you.'

Tweed returned to his Audi, parked round the corner. Paula had run ahead of him. Behind him he heard Reedbeck's barking yell.

'I'll remind you I'm in sole charge of this murder investigation . . .'

Paula had unlocked the Audi and Lisa dived out onto the pavement, started running towards Tweed. She stopped briefly, tucked a card in his top pocket. Her face was ashen but she managed something of a smile.

'I'm going to lock myself in my house, try and eat some breakfast. Thank you so much for your help . . .'

As she disappeared round the corner he heard Reedbeck bellowing. His manner was back to bullying.

'You're confined to your house, Miss Clancy. I'll be round later for a thorough interrogation.'

Tweed sat in his car behind the wheel. He made no attempt to start the engine. He was reading the printed card Lisa had given him. Her address was 77 Lynton Avenue. He turned the card over. She had written on the back, *Will wait here until you or Paula call me. Lisa.*

'And now,' Tweed said to Paula fiercely, 'if you'll loan me your mobile, I'm going to set in motion a volcanic eruption.'

Tweed pressed the buttons for Commander Buchanan's private number at the Yard, was relieved when Buchanan himself answered. Seated beside him, Paula clearly heard every word Buchanan used in reply. He was livid.

'I'll flay that Reedbeck alive. Leaving two bodies unguarded in the street! It's a scandal I sent him out there well over two hours ago, when the woman called to tell me about the bodies . . . No, she didn't leave a name. Sounded well spoken, rang off when I asked her for a name.'

'Why send a man like Reedbeck?' Tweed broke in.

'Shortage of staff. Only man available. Tweed, I know I've asked you for too much help over the past year . . .'

Tweed sighed. 'But you want me to involve myself in the case?'

'I want you to assume complete charge of the investigation.' Buchanan paused. 'I have to ask you to take on Reedbeck as your assistant. Working completely under your command. That I'll make bloody clear to him.'

'Why?' snapped Tweed.

'He has influence, which is why I was forced to agree to his working at the Yard. He was an inspector at a local police station in Hobartshire . . .'

'Hobartshire? I've just about heard of it. Where is it?'

Paula already had unfolded her map of Great Britain. She was pointing with an elegant finger. She nodded.

'It's all right, Roy,' Tweed said, 'Paula has located it.'

'It's in the middle of nowhere, the whole country,' Buchanan went on. 'I know your history is good. Remember centuries ago a few MPs had pocket boroughs they ruled like little kings? Hobartshire is still like that, controlled by a Lord Bullerton, who is a pal of Reedbeck's. Bullerton also dines with Reedbeck at his country house. Hence the manipulation of Reedbeck into my lap plus promotion to chief inspector. As Commander of the Anti-Terrorist Squad I can't waste time fighting them.'

'I'll take over the complete investigation. Hammer that into Reedbeck's thick head,' Tweed said grimly. 'Now I'm contacting Professor Saafeld. He'll be over here in fifteen minutes with his special vehicle. Tell Reedbeck that. Next we're off to Pine Street police station to find out just who Reedbeck has locked up on no evidence at all. You can reach me on Paula's mobile. You have the number. She's by my side. Goodbye . . .'

He called and explained the situation to Professor Saafeld. The pathologist confirmed he should arrive inside ten minutes, using his sirens.

'You may meet opposition at Pine Street,' Paula warned.

'I'll crush it.'

They drove out of the silence of Bexford Street into heavy traffic. Eventually, arriving at Pine Street, they saw a police motor cycle courier Tweed recognised. He jumped off his parked machine, ran to Tweed.

'This is for you, sir, from Commander Buchanan,' the courier explained, handing him a large sealed envelope. 'Don't bother about a receipt. I know you and I'll forge your name.'

'Good man.' Tweed was breaking the seals after sitting back in the passenger seat Paula had vacated. The envelope contained two official-looking documents, which he scanned quickly. He raised his eyebrows when he saw the signatures on both.

'Any trouble here and I'll clobber them,' he told Paula. 'You stay with me all the time.'

Pine Street station was an ugly new mass of concrete blocks with a crooked needle on top of the central gable. Inside, Tweed was confronted with a stubborn-faced uniformed policeman behind a reception counter protected with a screen of bars.

'You'll 'ave to wait. Sit over there. We're busy,' Stubborn informed him in a rasping voice.

'Read this document. I presume you can read? Lift this barrier – but first look at my identity folder. *Now!*'

Stubborn peered at the SIS folder. He swallowed after reading the document, and raised the barrier. 'Lumme,' he gasped, 'first time I've ever seen the signature of the Assistant Commissioner. Gather you want to see the murderer we locked up.'

'Watch your words,' Tweed snapped. 'And I need to interview him in complete privacy. With my assistant, Miss Grey.'

Stubborn pressed a button below his counter.

'They want to see the . . . prisoner Chief Inspector Reedbeck brought in. If they so decide, they have authority for him to be released into Mr Tweed's custody.'

'I'm Constable Merle Pardoe,' a uniformed policewoman informed them in a pleasant voice. She extracted a bunch of keys from inside her pocket. Not dangling from her belt where they could be snatched, Tweed noticed. As she unlocked a steel door he glanced at Paula, sending her a signal. He needed extra staff at Park Crescent.

Once they were the far side of the closed door, in a long deserted corridor, Paula reacted, smiling at Constable Pardoe.

'I may need to interview you about conditions here. Where is a good place we could meet if Mr Tweed decides he'd like me to do that?'

Without stopping, Pardoe took a card from her top pocket and scribbled something on the back, handed it to Paula. She paused before unlocking another steel door at a lower level.

'I shouldn't say it. That Sergeant, Wulgar, is bad enough but you are about to meet Frankenstein himself, a guard called Milburn. Staff were chosen by Chief Inspector Reedbeck.'

'Explains a lot,' Paula said to herself.

'He kept me on "for the moment", as he put it because I'd been here to clear up the place before it went on station. It was spotless after I'd chivvied up the cleaning ladies. Take a deep breath now.'

She used another key to open a third massive steel door down in the cells, told them they'd arrived and walked swiftly away. On the other side of the door their way was blocked by a six-foot-two giant.

'Milburn?' enquired Tweed.

'That's me.'

He had the build of an American quarterback, his wide chest and shoulders almost bursting out of his uniform. His large ugly face and icebreaker-like jaw exuded aggression.

'Is that the prisoner I've come to interview?' Tweed demanded.

'That's 'im.' He leered at Paula. 'Is this your girl? Or is she snooty like that Pardoe bit?'

'Which suggests,' Paula broke in, 'you tried to come on to her and she told you to get lost.' Her tone was icy. 'I wonder why?'

'Watch your dirty mouth,' Tweed warned him in a dangerously quiet voice. 'You're in the presence of a lady, like Miss Pardoe. Now shut up and open the cell door.'

The prisoner was a lean man, good looking, with long dark hair and a neatly trimmed moustache. He was settled on the only furniture in the cell, a long bed at the rear, perched against a foam pad serving as a pillow. His legs were carefully stretched along the bed and he wore a smart grey suit. A clean blue shirt was open at the collar, exposing a lean muscular neck. He glanced at Tweed and Paula, then switched his gaze to his well-polished walking shoes.

'The sod—' Milburn began then changed it as Tweed glared at him. 'The prisoner won't talk, hasn't uttered one word since they brought 'im in. No name. Nothing. I'll sort 'im out this evening,' he promised as he unlocked the cell door.

'Leave the door unlocked and open,' Tweed ordered as he entered the cell with Paula.

Watching Tweed's expression, Paula had the

impression sudden recognition was dawning. On the other hand the prisoner gazed at Tweed with no sign of recognition whatsoever. Tweed called over his shoulder.

'Milburn, I repeat, don't lock that door, we're leaving with the prisoner. You've had your orders from Sergeant Wulgar. And now you don't say a word.'

Tweed and Paula smiled at Merle Pardoe as she opened the door to the outside world. Tweed paused to speak to her.

'We do appreciate the courtesy you've shown us since we entered Dartmoor.'

'That's our duty, sir.'

'No, that's *your* duty, which you perform perfectly. No one else in this place.'

'Mr Tweed,' Wulgar called out as they were passing his counter, 'I need you to sign this document confirming the prisoner is now in your custody.'

'Sign it yourself,' Tweed rapped back as they walked on, leaving the station.

Outside, Tweed opened the rear door of the Audi, gestured to both Paula and the prisoner.

'The two of you ride in the back.'

As he was driving along the busy road he called out again to his passengers.

'Paula, meet ex-Inspector Dermot Falkirk, once stationed at Scotland Yard. Now I'm looking for a nice place which serves coffee and maybe sandwiches.'

2

'You must have recognized Tweed the moment we came into the cell,' Paula said to Falkirk. 'Yet you showed no sign you'd ever seen him before. Why?'

'I wasn't saying a word inside that place. Reedbeck may have had my cell wired.'

'But even earlier, when you were falsely arrested, you kept quiet.'

'Had to. Reedbeck made a colossal blunder. Arrested me on no evidence. Didn't recognize me until after his arrest. I've grown this moustache since I left the Yard and worked under him. Also my hair has grown very long. When he realized who I was it was too late – for him. He had set the wheels in motion, was too stupid to back off . . .'

'It took me a few moments to realize who you were,' Tweed admitted.

'What are you doing now?' Paula asked, using Tweed's technique of switching the topic suddenly to throw her target off balance.

'We're going back a couple of years. I started my own private investigation agency.'

'What's it called?'

'Eyes Only. Short and to the point . . .'

He paused as Paula's mobile buzzed. She answered and after a few words she handed it to Tweed. 'Professor Saafeld. Sounds urgent.'

'We'll be there in half an hour, maybe less,' Tweed said after listening briefly. 'He's puzzled,' he told Paula. 'If you're willing to cooperate with me on this case,' he said to Falkirk, 'you can come with us. Which client are you working for now?' he asked abruptly.

'Now you know a private detective never reveals the identity of his client,' Falkirk smiled engagingly. 'Part of the code.'

The Audi was stopped. The traffic wasn't moving. Tweed opened his door, called over his shoulder.

'We'll be here awhile. An accident with police cars. A huge tow-truck is grappling with a monster Cadillac. You won't be able to get into Saafeld's mortuary, Falkirk. I've just spotted Buchanan in a car three vehicles back. Both of you stay here . . .'

'Then I'll leave you in a minute,' Falkirk called back. 'Have an urgent appointment so I'll be able to get there early.'

'Refusing to tell us who your client is doesn't strike

me as my idea of cooperation,' Paula said sharply when Tweed had gone.

'Sorry, way of the world.'

'Another thing,' she persisted, 'private detectives always have to carry an identity folder and yet you hadn't anything on you when they searched you at Pine Street.'

'Reedbeck is a lousy searcher.' Falkirk grinned, opened his jacket, lifted the hem. Undoing an invisible zip fastener he extracted an identity folder, handed it to her. The photo of him was good and she saw he was forty years old.

'You need money too,' Falkirk went on.

From the same pocket he prised out a wad of folded banknotes. She guessed he must be carrying at least two hundred pounds. He must be doing well out of Eyes Only.

Tweed had lied when he told them he'd seen Buchanan. In his rear-view mirror he'd seen Harry following several vehicles behind him in his beat-up old grey Fiat. Stationary in the log jam, Harry jumped out, followed Tweed down a side street. A woman backed her car out of a resident's bay and drove off.

'You won't believe this,' the cockney began. 'Back at the office, earlier, I was coming in when I heard voices. The door wasn't closed properly. I heard what Lisa said about the people stalking her, then crept back up the stairs. Well, on your way with her to Lynton Avenue, with me keeping well back, she *was* followed. A hunchback first. He vanishes down an alley. When I've found an empty parking slot and run back to the alley he's gone. I hurtle down the empty alley into the next street. A woman dressed in black with a black veil walks past me. Carrying a large strong carrier bag from an expensive clothes shop.'

'Peculiar.' Tweed began talking quickly. 'I have a passenger in my car beside Paula.'

'Falkirk. Met him over two years ago. When you sent me down to the Yard with a sealed folder.'

'God, what a memory.'

'Has a 'tache and long hair since then.'

'Listen, Harry, he'll be leaving me shortly. Follow him to the end of the earth . . .'

'I can just turn the Fiat into that empty slot. If he walks I'll collect the car later. If he takes a cab I'll use the car.'

'Don't lose him.'

'You *are* talking to Harry Butler!'

The moment Tweed settled himself behind the wheel of his Audi, Falkirk opened his door on the pavement side. Squeezing Paula's arm, he paused to speak to Tweed.

'I'm off now. Pointless if I'm not allowed into the mortuary. Saafeld is right, of course. I'll keep in contact. Be good – if you can't do that, be careful. Cheerio . . .'

In his rear-view mirror Tweed saw Falkirk take the second empty taxi parked behind them. He was amused at his choice.

'Falkirk ignored the first empty cab, took the one behind it. He was worried I'd hired Harry to follow him.'

'Well, we've lost him anyway,' Paula said, now occupying the front passenger seat next to Tweed.

He smiled as the traffic suddenly started moving again. He told her about his conversation with Harry. When he reported his instructions Paula smiled.

'Falkirk may be smart but Harry's smarter. He'll never lose him.'

She went on to tell him about the trick with his identity folder and the money he was carrying. Tweed merely grunted, his mind elsewhere. As they reached Holland Park he turned down the winding cul-de-sac leading to Saafeld's HQ. There were other large private mansions vaguely visible behind trees coming into leaf. It had been a hard winter so the trees were flourishing late. He stopped in front of a pair of high wrought-iron gates let into a ten-foot-high wall, jumped out, used the speakphone set into a pillar to identify himself.

The gates opened, closed automatically behind them. They walked up a curving drive hemmed in by rhododendron bushes. A large white stone mansion came into view and Saafeld stood waiting by a massive open front door.

Professor Saafeld, the country's top pathologist, was of medium height, well built, thick white hair above a high forehead which suggested brain power. It was an impression reinforced by the sharpness of his eyes, which gazed unblinking at anyone he was talking to. He wore a smart blue bird's-eye suit and was in his late fifties. He hugged Paula, who had been to his HQ before.

'I'm not going to hug you,' he said with a grin at Tweed.

'Thank heavens for small mercies.'

'We'll go straight into the mortuary. I'm only at the first stage of my autopsy on the two ladies. Also,' he went on, 'I'm puzzled. Show you why . . .'

In front of a large steel door coated with white enamel he pressed buttons inside a security panel, pulled at the handle. The door opened and closed with an airlock's sucking sound. They descended a flight of stone steps into a small room which was very cold. Paula remembered the procedure as Saafeld opened a cupboard, handed each of them a white coat, a cap, a pair of white gloves and a pair of outsize canvas shoes. The moment they were dressed he pressed buttons in another security panel and a large steel door opened slowly. A unique odour drifted in the air, the odour of death. This time she was prepared for it as she adjusted her mask.

'You're getting used to it,' Saafeld said with a reassuring smile. He was not wearing a mask. 'I never do, but sometimes there's an element in the odour which tells me how they died . . .'

It was a large room with eight spotless metal-topped

tables equipped with encircling gutters. Saafeld skipped the length of the room to two more tables, occupied with bodies covered with white sheets. Paula was always amazed at Saafeld's agility: he moved like a twenty-year-old. A tall man clothed in white stood waiting.

'This excellent chap is Joffey, my new assistant. Been here six months. Joffey, meet our important visitors. Deputy Chief Tweed and his brilliant assistant Paula Grey. I'd say we're ready now . . .'

Paula tensed inwardly as Joffey lifted the nearest sheet. It was the woman who had lain nearest Lisa Clancy's house. Paula shuddered inwardly. The cuts had dug deeply into her flesh.

'Hatred on the killer's part,' Paula said softly.

'Or a determination neither would be recognizable,' Tweed commented.

At a nod from Saafeld, Joffey replaced the sheet, moved to the next table. He lifted the sheet clear of the head and neck again. The massacre of the face was just as ruthless on the other victim.

'In each case,' Saafeld explained, 'the killer cut the throat first with a very sharp knife. I suggest he came up behind them, grabbed their long hair, which you notice was dishevelled, hauled the head back, exposing the throat for a swift slash ear to ear. Probably only took seconds. What puzzles me is what kind of weapon he used to ruin their faces, to create the deep random squiggles. Hector might solve the problem – you can't put photos of those horrors in the papers asking if anyone knows them. Joffey, ask Hector to join us.'

'Hector?'

Paula was taken aback by the name. She made a major effort to compose her expression when Joffey opened a door at the rear. A very small tubby man bounced into the room. Humpty Dumpty, Paula said under her breath.

'May I introduce you to one of the cleverest men in the country,' Saafeld began. 'Meet Hector Humble.' He introduced the tubby little man to his guests. 'He can bring both those women back to how they looked in life.'

'Impossible!' Tweed burst out.

'I've studied the faces, sir,' Hector assured him. 'It can be done.' He tapped a large cardboard-backed envelope under his arm. 'I have photographed them as they are now. I must warn you,' he went on in his singsong voice, 'the job will cost you a fortune. Probably ten thousand pounds only payable if you're satisfied.' He began dancing round. 'I can see you're sceptical. Why not come with me to my work den. Just three side roads from here.'

'I strongly urge you to visit his work den,' Saafeld said.

Outside, Hector pointed to a large Mercedes parked beyond the Audi before he danced along the cul-de-sac towards it. His chubby face was all smiles.

'I'll lead the way. Leaving this close, turn left, then I'm the third turn-off on the left. My work den has a red metal cone over the chimney, in case you lose me . . .'

Dancing off down the cul-de-sac he paused at the front of his Merc. The rear of his car was facing the back of the Audi. In his rear-view mirror Tweed watched him fiddling with something.

'"In case you lose me,"' he quoted Hector ironically. 'In this traffic. Where does he think he is? Le Mans?'

At that moment Hector turned the Merc round and drove past them. Tweed stared. Paula shook with laughter. Tweed glared at her as he started his car.

'What's the matter with you?'

'Didn't you see? He's stretched white ribbon from the symbol on the bonnet back to each corner of his windscreen. People will think he's late collecting the bride and groom from their wedding!'

'Must be batty . . .'

'Or clever. Look what's happening.'

The Merc was swinging all over the place on the main road as other traffic stopped by the kerb. Hector was honking his horn gently and politely. A Rolls-Royce backed a few feet to let him through. Then Hector vanished.

Paula was checking side turnings on the left, counting them. Hector had called back as he left them that he was at Salty Close. Tweed was crawling behind traffic when Paula warned him.

'Next turning to the left. Salters Close . . .'

'I thought he said Salty Close.'

'He did.' She dug him gently in the ribs. 'Where's your sense of humour? Hector has one. And there's his work place on the right – complete with a red cone over the chimney. Don't look so grim – we got here. So did Hector, ahead of you.'

They walked up a short path to an oak front door which had three knockers, one very high up. Paula took out a coin, spun it and smiled at Tweed.

'I suspect Hector is full of tricks. Lift me so I can reach the top one.' She pointed to a sturdy wooden box beyond the step. 'That's for small visitors to stand on.'

Tweed hoisted her easily, holding her round her slim waist. She hammered the top knocker twice and Tweed lowered her to the step. The door opened quickly after the turning of two locks and the release of a heavy chain. Hector stood there, beaming.

He looked even stranger since he was wearing a pair of enormous large-lensed glasses. He pushed them back over his forehead and stared at Paula.

'That was you, clever girl. I know because you knocked lightly and didn't try to drive the knocker through the door. So come on in.' He was speaking quickly. 'I need the glasses when I'm working – these lenses have great magnification. I have started on your project,' he told Tweed.

After relocking the front door he led them down a narrow hall into a large room. Paula was startled –

there were wooden tables with various unusual tools neatly arranged, and shelves stacked with life-size featureless heads in smooth wood, some male, many female. The ceiling was a slab of thick glass providing plenty of light.

'My work den,' Hector explained. He wore a short white coat over his suit. 'The top knocker causes that red bulb to light up, tells me it's someone I know – not an estate agent wanting to tell me he could sell this place for a fortune.'

'Can I just wander round?' Tweed suggested. 'Never seen anywhere like this.'

'Wander, wander as you wish.' He took Paula gently by her arm. 'This is the most comfortable chair,' he went on, leading her to a leather armchair. For a moment he stared hard at her, then he nodded his head, turned his back on her and opened a cupboard.

Inside was an amazing collection of models of women's heads. He chose one, rejected it, chose another. Paula was suspicious. Hector placed it on a plinth on a wide shelf, opened another cupboard. Inside was a huge collection of wigs, also perched on plinths – blonde, jet black, brown. Selecting one with longish jet-black hair, he used a brush to create a glossy effect, arranged it on the plinth on the shelf. By now Paula was thoroughly suspicious. She waited for him to turn round but he still kept his back to her.

Finally he opened another cupboard, neatly arranged, took out an eye shadow, tested the colour on a sheet of cartridge, then applied it slowly above the eyeless head. His last act was to choose a lipstick, then apply that over the wooden lips. At that moment Tweed returned. For the first time Hector turned round, looked at Tweed.

'Well, what do you think of this?'

'Good God!' Tweed exclaimed. 'It's Paula.'

'I don't like it.' Paula had jumped up. She checked her watch. 'And he produced that in five minutes. You're not going to photograph it, I hope,' she said severely.

Hector looked disturbed. He ran forward and gently grasped her hand.

'I'm sorry. You have my word it will not be photographed – and within minutes of your leaving it will no longer exist.'

'Don't get upset,' she urged him in a softer voice. 'I just find it creepy. And you never looked at me.'

'I will confess,' he replied, his voice shaky, 'I could see you over there.'

He pointed to a large mirror attached to the far wall. There was something special about it. Her image was so clear. She managed to smile.

'You clever thing.'

Seeing he was still upset, almost had tears in his eyes, she kissed him lightly on one cheek.

'Time for us to go,' Tweed said briskly. 'My office will by now be in turmoil with both of us absent,' he fibbed. 'Hector, can you give me any idea when you'll let me have the photos?'

'So sorry, but I never predict that – I don't know. I assure you I will make it as quick as I can, for a double murder investigation.'

3

'They're all lying, the people we've met – either delib-erately or by omission. Not telling us what they know.'

'Who are they?' asked Paula.

Tweed had turned off the main road, and was head-ing north. His expression was determined. He listed who 'they' were.

'First, I'll check when Lisa anonymously phoned the Yard reporting the presence of the two bodies.'

'You really think it was her?'

'Who else? All the occupants of the other houses would be on holiday. Well off, they go abroad early to avoid the mobs on the beaches in July and August. Most of their curtains were closed.'

'Lisa is a very nervous person . . .'

'Not nervous enough to imply she didn't know either of the victims, living on either side of her. This is a very mysterious case. I know Sergeant Peabody and he's a good searcher. Yet he has reported no trace in either house of the victim's identity. No sign of ransacking by someone removing identity traces. *Most mysterious.*'

'Falkirk seemed straight enough.'

'No, he didn't. Just happened to be strolling along such a quiet street with two bodies lying on the steps. Coincidence? Don't believe in them.'

'I'm not thinking clearly,' she admitted.

'You were thrown by the extraordinary likeness of yourself Hector produced for my benefit.'

'*Your* benefit?'

'Mine,' Tweed replied. 'He sensed my scepticism about his work so he gave me a demonstration to impress me. Must say, I was very impressed.'

'Where are we going now? This looks like the street where the murders were committed.'

'It is. I'm going to put Miss Lisa Clancy through the verbal wringer.'

'Tweed here,' he said using Lisa's speakphone. 'Open the door. I have questions to ask you.'

'I'm very tired . . .'

'So am I. You have two options. Open the door or I'll call the police to open it. Then I'll escort you to Scotland Yard.'

'You sound so different.'

'The door.'

Within a minute they heard chains being removed, two locks turned. Lisa was wearing a velvet jacket and trousers. Expensive. She gave Tweed a flashing smile, ignored Paula as though she did not welcome her presence. She led them along a hall with a blue fitted carpet to a staircase. On one side of the hall was an antique refectory table on which was perched a Ming vase. Paula smelt money.

At the top of the staircase they entered a living room overlooking the street. Heavy net curtains covered the windows and heavy red floor-to-ceiling curtains were drawn back. Lisa asked them to sit down on a couch close to an antique table, then seated herself in a tall carver chair opposite. Casually she took off her jacket, exposing a low-cut blouse.

Paula waited to see how Tweed would handle her. It was obvious that Lisa was trying to soften him up.

'The first thing for you to do,' Tweed barked, 'is to put on your jacket again and button it to the neck. The first question is how well did you know the two victims – living on either side of you?'

'Hardly knew them at all,' she replied sullenly as she put on her jacket and buttoned it up.

'You're expecting me to believe you never spoke to them once?'

'I didn't say that. Once I was coming back late from work in the dark. Well ahead of me, the one round the corner was walking home by herself. When I reached her she was still outside struggling to open her door. I stopped, asked if she had a problem. She said, without turning round, her lock sticks, that it was the recent wet weather and the door had dropped. She got the key to turn at that moment, went inside without a word to me.'

'Did she know the other victim?'

'I think so. I saw them coming home together late one evening. Probably been to the theatre . . .'

'And you maintain you were friendly with neither of them?'

'I thought I'd made that perfectly clear,' she snapped.

Her whole personality had changed. Her face was hard, her voice hostile. She began to tremble, twisting her hands clasped together in her lap.

'Do your parents live nearby?' he persisted.

'Hardly,' she snapped again. 'Both were killed in a traffic accident three years ago . . .'

'Where did you spend your childhood? Where were you born?'

'Cutwick, a small village in Hampshire,' she said quickly as though she'd been waiting for this question.

'I see you've had the locks changed on your front door. A Banham and a Chubb.'

'Wouldn't you! – if you'd had the experience I've had?' She stood up, her expression murderous. 'And, Mr Tweed, I've had just about enough of you.'

Tweed stood up and Paula followed suit. His manner also changed; he was smiling and his voice was sympathetic.

'It's just that I'm worried about you. Do you have to go to work today?'

'I've phoned Rumble, Crowther and Nicholas, told them I'm not well, that I think I'm coming down with the flu.'

'Do you have to go out to shop? If not, may I suggest that you stay in the house if possible.'

'I'll show you my fridge. It's stacked with enough food to last me ten days.' Her voice became sarcastic. 'I wouldn't want you to worry about me. Now, I'll show you both out.'

'If there's a development, we might have to come back.'

'Don't bother . . .'

She led the way down the staircase, said not another word as they left and stood on the street. They heard her dealing with both new locks. Paula sighed.

'I think you were pretty tough on her.'

'She's still lying. I hoped to break her down.'

As he spoke, a Rolls-Royce glided round a distant corner, drove slowly towards them in the stately fashion a Rolls should be driven. The uniformed chauffeur slowed down even more as he cruised past them, and Lisa's house. The rear windows were heavily tinted, making it impossible to see the passenger, who appeared to be peering at them. Reaching the corner beyond which the second victim's house was located it continued its leisurely cruise, vanished.

'That was curious,' Paula commented. 'I memorized the plate number. I'll phone Swansea, find out who owns it.'

'We'll get back to Park Crescent,' Tweed decided. 'I didn't like the way that Rolls behaved, I want to know who that passenger was – the one who prefers no one can identify him. Another mystery, I suspect.'

4

Arriving back at Park Crescent, they found Tweed's spacious office occupied by all the members of his team, with the exception of Harry Butler. Bob Newman, once the most famous international reporter on the planet, sat the wrong way round on a wooden chair, arms folded on the back. Tallish and well built, in his early forties, he was good-looking, was often glanced at by elegant women in the street. He slapped Paula on the arm as she hurried to her corner desk.

'Busy, busy lady,' he chaffed her.

Leaning against the wall by Paula's desk, his normal position, a very tall lean man was smoking a cigarette in a holder. He wore an Armani suit; his smile was cynical, his hair dark, well brushed. This was Marler, reputed to be the deadliest marksman in Europe. He was in his late thirties.

Pete Nield, Butler's 'partner in crime', was also smartly clad in a white suit and shirt, wearing a Chanel tie. Amiable, as always, his hair was flaxen with a neatly trimmed moustache. Almost as good a 'shadow' as his partner, he was also in his late thirties.

Tweed wasted no time. Seating himself behind his desk he told everyone what had happened so far. It was his policy that all of them should know what the case was about, starting with the discovery of the two women's murders, and ending with the peculiar appearance of the Rolls.

'So where are we?' drawled Marler.

'Nowhere,' Tweed said bluntly. 'As yet no connections, no leads.'

'Can't imagine you letting us all just sit here,' Marler observed shrewdly.

'Wait a minute,' Paula called out.

She had been huddled over her phone, one hand in an ear to block out Tweed's powerful voice.

'Everyone shut up. I may have something . . .'

'Well,' said Monica from her desk behind the door, 'I've just had an urgent phone call from Harry. No time to switch it to you, Tweed. He is following Falkirk's car miles away. He reports Falkirk's car broke down, Falkirk called the AA, who have just arrived. Harry drove into a nearby field to get into cover.'

'But where is he?' Tweed asked irritably.

'In the middle of nowhere, then he ended the call.'

'Very helpful. Could be Devon, Norfolk, anywhere . . .'

'Harry knows what he's doing,' Pete Nield said quietly. 'He sounds close to Falkirk at the moment. Probably because that car broke down. You've always said leave decisions to the man in the field – he knows the situation better than you do.'

'Absolutely right. I'd just hoped we had a break. Sorry.'

'Anyone want to listen to me?' Paula enquired sharply.

'Go ahead,' Tweed urged, placing a hand close to one ear.

'First,' Paula began, 'I phoned Swansea with the index number. The Rolls we saw is a company car. Belongs to Otranto Oil. Doesn't get us far. So I phoned your pet accountant and friend, Keith Kent. Asked him about Otranto.'

'That was smart,' Tweed said quickly.

'Keith knows a lot about them. The owner is Neville Guile, a ruthless man who has built up Otranto into a major powerful complex – by buying up small oil companies. Methods he's used are very open to question, including blackmail and worse. Has three Rolls, two company and one his own. Now, listen, his HQ is in Finden Square . . .'

'Where?' asked Tweed.

'I know it. Finden Square is small, hidden away not so far from Bexford Street and Lynton Avenue, where the murders took place. It's an oasis of peace amid the turmoil of London. I'd like to check it out.'

'Come with you,' offered Marler. 'This Neville

Guile sounds a dangerous character. And he may have seen you if he was in the back of that Rolls.'

'I'd welcome your company,' Paula said. 'Let's get moving.'

As soon as they had left Tweed stared at Newman from behind a fresh pile of red files containing more overseas agents' reports just delivered from Communications. Newman smiled back at Tweed's glare.

'Anything for me to do?'

'Yes. Put on that shabby mac you keep for the East End. Go down there, meet your contacts. Ask if there are rumours about any imminent operation.'

'What sort of operation?'

'How do I know?'

'What's the matter with him?' Newman whispered to Monica as he took his shabby raincoat from a cupboard. 'He's like a bear with a sore head.'

'Won't last long,' Monica said soothingly. 'He's frustrated because he's no lead, no connection established with this murder investigation.'

'Then let's hope something breaks soon,' Newman said as he left the office to pursue what he regarded as a futile task.

Marler stared as they entered Finden Square. All four sides were occupied by a stately block of Adam-style terraced houses. Steps led up to each artistically designed front door. At each corner the blocks were separated by a side street to the outside world. In the middle was an oblong garden with evergreen trees and shrubs, surrounded with a high railing.

'And I never knew this existed,' he marvelled.

'You don't walk, exploring, like I do in quiet times,' Paula remarked. 'You spend your spare time sitting in pubs, pretending to listen for information,' she chaffed him.

'It's so incredibly quiet. No one about.'

'That's our target,' she said, pointing through a gap in the foliage to a corner building directly opposite them. 'See the huge letter O poised on a mast on the roof? Looks to be made of perspex – probably illuminated by night.'

She had just spoken when the front door opened. Marler put a hand on her shoulder, pressed her down into a crouch while he joined her, now concealed by shrubbery. She peered through a small gap, whispered a running commentary.

'Uniformed servant emerging from front door, carrying costly leather luggage. A Rolls-Royce has pulled up at bottom of the steps. Heavily tinted windows in back. Sophisticated radio system on roof. Mr Neville Guile is well organized. Luggage stacks in boot. Chauffeur behind wheel now gazing at front door. Probably waiting . . . Yes, I was right. A tall slim man in perfectly cut suit walking down to door which the chauffeur has opened for him, standing to attention.'

'What does Guile look like?' Marler whispered.

'Too far away for precise description. Long, lean,

could be in his forties. He's stopped to speak to the chauffeur.'

To her astonishment they could hear every word the passenger said. The voice was high-pitched, cultured.

'Jordon, we will stop halfway there until we have more news. Find a good hotel in Oaks-ford. A reasonable halfway house.'

'Oaks-ford,' repeated Marler. 'Where's that?'

'Oxford. It's the way he talks. Rolls about to leave . . .'

'Then so are we. He could drive this way and see us. No, not by the side road we entered.' He grasped her arm. 'Down the alley behind us . . .'

He hustled her across the road into a narrow alley, the like of which Paula had never seen before. The floor was tiled with clean blue slabs. No sign of rubbish, of the unpleasant objects found in so many London alleys. Finden Square extended its air of exclusivity to the main street. As they emerged from the alley, Marler took Paula by the arm, hustled her to the parked Saab he'd borrowed from Pete Nield.

'What's the rush for?' she protested.

'So we can be clear of this main street in case that Rolls is coming this way . . .'

Without opening the door for her he slid behind the wheel. It was fortunate he'd parked with the car pointed away from the exit out of Finden Square. Paula, seated beside him, turned round as Marler accelerated.

They had reached the end of the main road when,

turning a corner and plunging into an inferno of traffic, Marler cut off a cab. The driver yelled at him, honked his horn.

'Cab drivers think they own London streets, which they do,' Marler commented. 'But no one cuts me off.'

'You were so right,' Paula told him. 'Just before we turned I caught a glimpse of that Rolls. It *was* turning this way.'

'So where to now?'

'Back to Park Crescent. I want to tell Tweed what we saw.'

Meanwhile, Newman was on the move, heading for the East End. Despite the traffic he reached the district quickly.

He was noted for his fast and skilful driving, sliding through gaps other drivers would hesitate to tackle. He struck lucky, finding his four informants quickly in the pubs where they spent their afternoons.

The third informant, small and tubby as a barrel from the beer he consumed, shook his head, gave the same answer as the previous two contacts.

'I ain't 'eard nothing on the go – and nothing planned. It's very quiet round these parts . . .'

Newman thanked Tubby and gave him a ten-pound note to keep him sweet. He had only one more contact, just along the street, if he was there. This was the most astute of all his network of informants.

He bought an apple off a stall, and was chewing it when he walked into the Pig's Trotters. His informant was a tall thin man with sleepy eyes which missed nothing. Newman put the same question to him.

'Your timing is uncanny,' said Mr Merton, as he liked to be known, 'and I'd advise you not to look at the bar yet. Someone just came in. Munch that apple slowly – gives you a reason for sitting 'ere.'

Merton was comparatively well educated, but could talk cockney like a native. He sipped his glass of brandy, his favourite, then spoke again.

'Something is up – and the something is ordering champagne at the bar. Name of Lepard – father was French, mother English. Committed at least two murders already – one here, t'other in Paris. Escaped conviction both times on a technicality. Word is, he's been hired for a potential end job.' 'End job' was the new slang for a murder assignment.

'Any idea of the target, Mr Merton?' Newman enquired.

'Not a whisper. He's contacted some pretty ugly thugs to stand by for detailed instructions. A load of money has changed hands to keep them ready. May I suggest you shove off – Lepard is about to bring his champagne over to the table near us which just became available.'

Newman slipped Mr Merton a folded twenty-pound note, stood up, walked towards the door, still munching his apple. He didn't like the look of Lepard at all. The killer, wearing an expensive leather jacket and corduroy slacks, moved with a certain agility. His yellow eyes darted everywhere, scanning the whole room. A cadaverous face was softened by his well-shaped chin and a pleasant smile as he nearly knocked over a seated customer's glass of beer. His right hand grabbed the glass, prevented it spilling as he apologized.

Newman had seen all this in a wall mirror as, hunched down in his ancient raincoat, he padded slowly to the door and into the street. He was having trouble assessing Lepard. Outside he hailed a cab, asked to be taken to Euston Road. No point in mentioning Park Crescent in this area.

Dusk was falling as Paula and Marler entered Tweed's office. Paula immediately gave Tweed a brief description of what they had witnessed in Finden Square. Her chief liked terse reports.

'You're thinking of the Rolls which cruised past us when we were standing outside the double murder location,' he suggested.

'Yes, I am.'

'Did you get the plate number of the Rolls driving away from Otranto's HQ?'

'No, I couldn't. Only saw the car's side parked.'

'Then it's a guess, not evidence?'

'My instinct rather than a guess,' she countered.

'And,' Marler intervened, 'in the past Paula's instinct has so often proved to be right.'

'True,' Tweed agreed. He lit one of his rare ciga-
rettes. 'We have several threads but none of them ties
with the others . . .'

He stopped speaking as Newman opened the door,
walked across the room, perched on the edge of
Paula's desk next to Marler. He opened both hands in
a negative gesture, then reported his experience inside
the Pig's Trotters. He concluded with a shrug.

'Doesn't get us any further, does it?'

'You sound confused about this character Lepard,'
Tweed told him.

'Well, if he is a killer he has good manners, which
doesn't add up.'

'I've remarked before,' Tweed said amiably, 'that I
never cease to be fascinated by the complexity of
human nature, the mixture of good and evil in one
man – or woman. You explained he was of mixed
parentage. Some of these professional killers have egos
as big as the Ritz. The strange name has sinister
undertones. Le could be part of a French name, Pard
might be short for Pardoe – might be his mother's
maiden name.' He placed his hands behind his neck.
'It's another thread, floating in the wind.'

'So where do we go from here?' asked Paula.

'First, I suggest we all go home early, get a good
night's sleep. Who knows? I need a very positive lead.
Could come tomorrow.'

Tweed had no idea that the following morning the
investigation would explode in their faces.

50

5

Tweed arrived early at Park Crescent the next day, to find his whole team in his office, again with the exception of Harry Butler. As he hung up his camel-hair coat he glanced through the windows towards Regent's Park, which was bathed in sunlight. Another glorious May day. Monica leaned forward as he sat at his desk.

'You have a visitor in the waiting room downstairs. A Hector Humble.'

'Why park him in that dreary room?'

'He preferred not to invade your office until you arrived. He was quite firm about it.'

'Invite him up immediately.' Tweed sighed. 'He's come to warn me the photos of the two murdered women won't be ready for weeks.'

A clatter of feet on the stairs, the door opened,

Hector bounced into the room. His jacket was open and underneath he was clad in a waistcoat of many colours, all tasteful.

'Love your waistcoat,' Paula called out. 'Really unique.'

'Got it in the Old Kent Road. Half price – it had been displayed for weeks.'

Under his right arm he clutched two cardboard-backed envelopes. He was still blushing at Paula's praise, shyly accepted Monica's offer of coffee. He eased his rounded body into the chair Tweed, standing up, had gestured towards after shaking hands.

'Done it,' he said with an air of triumph. 'Worked through the night. Got absorbed. Knew you needed them urgently.'

Diving into the thicker envelope he produced a batch of photos. He spread two copies in front of Tweed, who stared in disbelief. He knew he was looking at glossy prints of the two murdered women as they had appeared alive. Even their long hair falling to their shoulders looked real.

The whole team gathered round the desk. Paula peered over his shoulder. She pursed her lips as she made her remark.

'They were both beautiful. We've got to get the swine who ruined them.'

'You have seven copies,' Hector went on. 'Don't look now inside this envelope. It will upset you. They're copies of how they looked before I rebuilt their faces. Just for your files.'

52

'But eventually,' Newman said fiercely, 'to show the jury when we've dragged the killer into court by his heels.'

The door opened and Howard, the Director, strolled in. He was a tall man with the beginnings of a stout stomach. He was perfectly dressed in a new grey Armani suit, pristine white shirt, cuffs shot beyond the sleeves, exposing gold cufflinks. An Hermès tie decorated the shirt front. Normally amiable, he had a serious expression as Tweed showed him the photos.

'Hector has performed a miracle. I told you about him before I went home last night.'

'Well, write out Mr Humble the cheque I approved.'

Tweed already had his chequebook out, was filling it in for ten thousand pounds. Hector protested.

'I quoted too much. Seven or eight would be most acceptable.'

'A deal is a deal,' Tweed insisted, writing in the originally agreed amount.

Howard picked up the photos of both women as they had been in life. He sighed.

'I'd like to have taken either lady to dinner . . .' He gulped. 'God! That was in the worst taste. I do apologize. I'm off back to my office.' He held out his large pink hand.

'Mr Humble, I've seen the work of experts in other fields but words fail me to express my admiration for your quite unique skill.'

He hurried from the office, still embarrassed by his

53

remark. Hector swallowed the rest of the coffee Monica had brought him, stood up, the cheque in his wallet. He grasped hold of Paula, kissed her on both cheeks.

'You're such a nice lady,' he murmured, blushing.

He darted out of the room before Paula could decide how to react. Tweed was sorting the photos into pairs, each pair comprising one photo of each murdered woman. He instructed Paula as the others returned to their desks.

'Every member of the team must have a copy.' He raised his voice. 'But everyone must be discriminating as to who sees them. Under no circumstances are you to reveal both women were murdered. It's identification of the victims that is holding up the investigation.'

'So not in the newspapers,' Newman suggested.

'Last place on earth,' Tweed replied emphatically.

'Well,' Newman insisted, 'this morning's *Clarion* has a big splash headline. It's my top newspaper friend, of course, Drew Franklin. Show him, Paula.'

TWO UNIDENTIFIED SOCIETY
WOMEN MURDERED
KILLER CUT THEIR THROATS. BEWARE!

Tweed looked up at Paula, who had spread the front page across his desk. Lower down on the same page something had been cut out. Tweed didn't waste time reading Franklin's lurid prose as he asked his question.

'Among the few people who knew about this crime, who would be your choice for the informant who accepted a bundle of cash to call Franklin – probably from a public phone box?'

'Roadblock,' she said promptly. 'Chief Inspector Reedbeck.'

'My choice too, although we'd never prove it. And something was cut out lower down. What was it?'

'Archie MacBlade is back in town after weeks abroad.'

'I've just about heard the name.'

'MacBlade is just about the most successful oil prospector on the planet,' Newman broke in. 'Back from Brunei, the oil-rich nation in the Far East. Controlled by the Sultan, perhaps the richest man in the world. MacBlade prospected in the jungle, brought up the most gigantic gusher ever seen there. The Sultan is probably three times richer than he was before.'

'I only cut this out because I was impressed by the picture of him. Struck me as a man of exceptional character.'

Tweed glanced at the cutting she'd pushed in front of him. He agreed with her estimate. The photograph was of a man with shaggy hair, piercing eyes under bushy brows, a Roman nose, a shaggy moustache and a wide mouth, below that a strong jaw. He had a pleasant smile. Tweed nodded, pushed the cutting back to her.

'I agree,' he said in a bored voice, 'but it's nothing to do with our present problem . . .'

The phone rang. Monica picked it up, listened, looked excited as she pointed to Tweed's phone.

'You might want to take this call. It's Harry.'

'Great to hear from you,' Tweed began. 'Where the devil are you? Hobartshire? Could you repeat that?'

Paula had already returned to her desk with her cutting. She hauled out a map from a desk drawer, waited.

It was a long conversation. Most of the time Tweed was scribbling data on a pad. Occasionally he said, 'Are you sure?' then he went on scribbling. Finally he asked, 'If Paula and I left now could we get there by lunchtime?'

'Yes, we could,' Paula called out.

'Did you say Gunners Gorge? Funny name,' Tweed commented.

'Got it,' Paula called out again. 'Small town on the River Lyne.'

'Can anyone hear this?' Tweed asked. 'Oh, you're on your mobile in a field. Sounds secure enough. If that's all, Paula and I will be starting out in five minutes. You've done well, Harry. Exceptionally well. See you . . .'

Tweed replaced the phone. His expression concealed the relief, the excitement he was feeling. He looked round the room at the members of his team.

'I sense this is the breakthrough we've been patiently waiting for. Patiently? Didn't apply to me. I apologize to all of you for my flashes of temper yesterday. Now,

Harry. He has tracked Falkirk to – of all places – Hobartshire. To what he called the weirdest of small towns – Gunners Gorge. He's booking suites for Paula and me at a good hotel, the Nag's Head. All the data is on this pad, which I'll leave with Monica. If I need reinforcements, you all have Paula's mobile number. Use that if something happens down there . . .'

As he was finishing speaking he jumped up, put on his camel-hair coat. Paula had already picked up two suitcases kept for emergency departures, one for herself, one for Tweed. She was striding to the door when Tweed relieved her of his own case and Pete Nield spoke.

'You don't know what you're walking into. I suggest you travel in the second Audi parked at the back. The one with armourplate on the body and armoured glass in the windows. Harry has souped up the engine.'

'Good thinking. I agree,' Tweed replied.

'I'll come down the back way with you – I've got the keys,' Pete added.

'Then,' Paula remarked, 'with the Audi the wrong people associate with us left parked out at the front they'll think we're still here.'

'More good thinking,' Tweed agreed.

Paula took the wheel, saying she knew the route. After crawling through the dense traffic of London, she drove faster through the suburbs, then accelerated as they reached the countryside. They were on a wide country road and Paula sighed with pleasure.

'Oh, this is wonderful. Away from the stench of petrol, the noise, young girls with mobiles pressed to their ears who walk into you, the pointless rush and bustle.'

'And the scenery,' Tweed added.

On either side were hedges in leaf, their twigs festooned with bright yellow honeysuckle. Through the gaps they saw endless slopes of green grass, copses of trees perched on isolated hillocks.

Above them the sun blazed down out of a clear duck-egg-blue sky. A large passenger plane had flown to a great height, was still climbing. Tweed pointed towards it as it changed direction, heading west.

'Look at what they're leaving behind, an earthly paradise.'

'Could be heading for the Bahamas,' Paula suggested. 'Those yacht basins crammed with private boats, the narrow streets choked with shoppers. No, thank you . . .'

As they kept heading roughly north-eastward Paula occasionally used a motorway. Overtaking, overtaking, overtaking. Back into the slow lane, then up a slip road, leaving the torrent of huge trucks and fast cars behind. Back into countryside.

'Where is Hobartshire?' Tweed enquired.

'Middle of nowhere. Least populated county. Not one city – inhabited by people with large estates who hunt for exercise.'

'Sounds like large parts of Britain used to be.'

'I gathered from a girl friend once it's just that.'

The scenery changed as they crossed from one county to the next. They passed an area of massive white rocks; here and there men with machines worked quarries. Then the road took them into a forest so dense and dark it blotted out the sun. Emerging from the forest, fertile and gently rolling grass-covered hills lay on either side. Tweed checked the time.

'We should be nearly there, shouldn't we?'

'The man's a genius,' said Paula and laughed. 'Look at that road sign,' she suggested as she slowed to a crawl.

The larger than usual metal sign carried a message, a very clear message.

HOBARTSHIRE

BEHAVE YOURSELVES HERE

POLICE

'Something tells me we might not be welcome in this neck of the woods,' Tweed remarked. 'We have just entered the bailiwick of Lord Bullerton.'

6

They drove on, with glimpses of rolling green slopes when gaps in the tall hedges gave them a view. They came to a point where the road descended into a village. Paula drove slowly now, staring.

'Funny sort of place,' she commented. 'No sign of a gorge.'

The village was strange. On either side of the narrowed road was a continuous line of old terraced cottages with white stone walls. Each cottage had a bright blue front door and tiny dormer windows in its low cramped roof. There was no one about and the place seemed eerie.

They arrived at a cottage on their left which had a bright red front door. On her hands and knees an old woman in a black coat was scrubbing fiercely at a stone step which, as far as Tweed could see, was as already white as snow. Paula stopped the car.

'Might get some information from her if she's the chatty type,' Tweed said.

The old lady stood straight up with surprising speed, dropped her scrubbing brush. She stared straight at them with alert eyes under a lined brow.

'I'm Mrs Grout,' she snapped. 'Who be 'ee?'

Tweed decided to try impressing her from the start. He produced his identity folder, held it up, then put it away. She was quick and there was nothing wrong with her eyesight.

'Deputy Chief, but not with the police is my guess.'

'Maybe a little more powerful,' Tweed said smiling.

'Come up a bit late to check on the murder of Lady Bullerton. Going to put the wind up Pit Bull?'

'Pit Bull? Sounds like a savage animal.'

'Which is what he is. You don't call 'im that to 'is face. He would find some way of running you out of 'Obartshire. He's got 'imself made Chief Constable by suckin' up to powerful folk in Lunnon.'

'So how would he run someone he didn't like here out of the county?'

'Well,' she began, 'a few years ago Pit Bull bought up the Village. That's what it's called. Cottages were on short leases, which 'e renews when they ends. Contracts were drawn up so that he could throw tenants out at a moment's notice. But before he bought the Village I'd 'ad a legacy from an aunt. Used it to buy my cottage. Means 'e can't tell me what to do. He was mad as an 'atter when Fingle, his local lawyer, missed it.'

'Why are all the doors painted bright blue?' Tweed wondered.

'It's in the leases for all other cottagers. Doors must be painted blue.' She chuckled. 'To show I'm independent I painted mine red. He's in a rage but can't do anything about it. So there!'

'You did mention,' Tweed said casually, 'that Lady Bullerton had been murdered. By whom and how do you know?'

'Saw it 'appen with my own two eyes and me binocs. Standing outside the Nag's Head I was. Sees movement up by Aaron's Rock at top of gorge. It were Lady Bullerton wearing her wings. We all 'as our funny ideas. She thought she could fly.'

Paula discreetly checked her watch. This was getting a bit much. To her surprise Tweed continued the conversation.

'What sort of a lady was she?'

'Very posh. Very clever. She could add up so many figures *and* do wonderful 'broidery. Made the wings herself. I sees 'er pushed over the edge. Down she drops through a hundred-and-fifty-foot waterfall into the river. Floatin' she was when I dashed into the Nag's Head, told Bert Bowling, landlord. Bert's quick – rushes out, tears off shoes and waistcoat, dives in. He gets 'er back onto the bank. Dr Margoyle appears, tries to 'elp 'er. Too late. She's drowned, poor thing.'

'You said you saw her pushed over,' Tweed persisted gently. 'You actually saw who did that to her?'

'Well . . . no,' she admitted reluctantly. 'Aaron's Rock hid who did her in. She was standing well back from a rock platform. Took me up there once in 'er car. "Don't ever go near the edge, Elsie. I don't," she says to me. I climbed up there a day later, crept under police tape. Platform was covered with blood. They cleaned that up.'

'Was there a strong wind that day?' asked Paula.

'Not even a bit of breeze.'

'The police would check it out,' Tweed suggested. 'How long ago was this tragedy?'

'Something over six years ago. Inspector Reedbeck said it was an accident.'

'Gave me a bit of a jolt when she mentioned Reedbeck,' Tweed remarked as they drove on past the Village and down a steep hill. Mrs Grout had pointed the direction to Gunners Gorge. 'Then I remembered Buchanan had told me he had been in charge of some local police station up here.'

'I think the old dear is round the bend,' Paula commented.

'She certainly provided some information – or misinformation – but we'll know when we talk to Harry.'

He turned a bend on the level now and an awesome sight spread out before them. Paula sucked in a deep breath. Gunners Gorge was a small town on both sides of the river. In the near distance a massive granite gorge sheered up on both sides of a churning

64

waterfall at least twenty yards wide. A turmoil of river water surged over the summit between granite boulders, plunging in a menacing volume far down into a raging pool between two roads on either bank. As they drove slowly towards the Nag's Head, which had a sign projecting with a horse's head, Paula suddenly said:

'Could you stop a minute? I've never seen anything like this.'

Tweed stopped. They both got out to stretch stiffened legs as Paula pointed at the steep hillsides rising up from both banks of the River Lyne. Old but expensive-looking houses perched above each other occupied the slopes. All were built of granite, which gave the small town a grim atmosphere.

'See,' Paula went on, 'no roads link them up the slopes. Just endless flights of stone paved steps. You'd have to be fit to live here – climbing all those steps.'

Tweed took out his powerful pair of compact binoculars. He studied low buildings with thatched roofs dotted at intervals at the top of the ridges. Each had a large single door.

'I think they've got garages on the crest-line, large ones with power-operated doors. Must be a road we can't see running along the top.'

'Then Heaven help people living in the houses just above this road.'

'That will be reflected in the price,' Tweed said with a smile. 'Let's get moving. Time for lunch. I could eat a horse.'

'Then we're staying at the right place.' Paula chuck-led. 'The Nag's Head . . .'

What added to the disturbing atmosphere was that there were no other people about. Tweed drove in under an arch to the car park. Almost concealed in a corner they saw Harry's Fiat. A jovial, strong-looking man wearing a green apron met them as they entered.

'Would you be the two visitors someone booked two suites for?'

'We would,' Tweed replied.

'I'm Bert Bowling, I own this place,' he explained as Tweed signed the register in their correct names. Tweed then asked his question.

'Could you tell me how to get to where Lord Bullerton lives?'

'Go back along the road you came in on. Just before you reach the Village there's a turn-off on your left, takes you right to his estate.'

'Thank you.'

'Poor old basket,' the landlord continued. 'He's had a lot of bad luck. Dines here quite often in the Silver Room . . .'

'What sort of bad luck?'

'First his wife slips over the edge of Aaron's Rock at the top of the falls. Plunges right down the gorge. Old Mrs Grout saw her go – down the hundred-and-fifty-foot drop. Mrs Grout comes rushing in here, so I charge out, dive into the river. I can see her body floating half below the surface with her wings flat on her back. I bring her ashore and a quack staying here tries to bring her round. No good. She's gone.'

'Did you say "wings"?'

'A very intelligent and balanced lady she was. But we all have our quirks. Used to say she could fly, but I know she didn't really believe it.'

'How long ago was this?'

'Over six years ago.'

'You did say,' Tweed began thoughtfully, 'Lord Bullerton had a lot of bad luck. Was there something else?'

'Well, yes. About a year ago his two – no, three – eldest daughters walked out on him. Stupid people spread nasty rumours that he used to beat them up. There are people who don't like him.'

'Did he ever hear from them?'

'Just a postcard from Nancy, who went to Canada. Another from Petra, who pushed off to Australia. Nothing from Lizbeth. You would like lunch in the Silver Room? I'll organize it . . .'

The Silver Room was on the first floor, as were their suites. The room could have graced a good London hotel with its oak-panelled walls and tables set well apart, covered with expensive white tablecloths. A cheerful waitress with chubby red cheeks appeared as soon as they were seated.

'Mr Bowling,' she informed them, 'said you were important and I must look after you especially well.'

'Don't know about being important,' Tweed said with a smile. He took one of the menus she offered as she handed another to Paula. 'We're the only ones having lunch,' he remarked. 'Have you anyone else staying here?'

'Just one gentleman by himself in Room One. Lean and restless he is. Never a smile. Never looks at me. Has something on his mind, I'd say. And I saw that Inspector Reedbeck in the hall. Used to be in charge of our police station. Saw him studying the hotel register late last night when Mr Bowling was down in the cellar. Cheek, I thought. Doesn't belong in Gunners Gorge any more. Sorry, I'm chattering too much but there's something about you which makes folk want to talk to you. Back in a minute when you've had time to decide . . .'

'She's fallen for you,' Paula teased him.

'Let's get on with lunch. I want to call on Lord Bullerton.'

They were downstairs about to leave when the landlord appeared full of apologies.

'I'm afraid I misled you about His Lordship. He still has two younger daughters living with him at Hobart House. And a twenty-year-old son called Lance. He'd been trying for years to get a son to carry on the line. Now he seems to have lost his enthusiasm for the idea. And I fear I also misled you about Lizbeth.'

'In what way?' Paula enquired.

'She didn't walk out with her elder sisters. They think she was drowned swimming in the river. Water was rough that day but Lizbeth was a strong swimmer.' He pushed a lock of grey hair away from his face. 'Odd thing about that. She was untidy, just threw her clothes off her swimsuit. Yet they were found neatly piled on the grass.'

'And her body was never found?' suggested Tweed.

'Could have been swept miles downstream. Time flies. Checked my diary. I told you it was over six years ago when Lady Bullerton went down the gorge. It was nineteen years ago. A year after the birth of Lance. Sorry about that.'

'Forget it. Doesn't matter.'

'There's a path across the grass opposite this hotel. Leads to a stone His Lordship personally had erected. Chose the wording himself. Mustn't hold you up like this.'

'What do you think of all that?' Tweed asked as he drove the Audi back the way they had come in.

'My head's in a whirl. All that information surging in. And Mrs Grout said Lady Bullerton had gone down the falls six years ago. Now Bowling, having said the same thing, corrects it to nineteen years ago.'

'Mrs Grout has most of her marbles but at that age memory can play tricks . . .'

'Funny that Bowling also said six years ago to start with.'

They had entered the Village and Tweed turned left down a lane bordered by high impenetrable hedges. No sign of Hobart House. There was a sudden loud report and the glass of the window next to Tweed was starred – but the glass remained intact.

'That was a bullet,' Paula hissed. 'Aimed at you.'

Tweed accelerated, risking that there was nothing round the next bend. Paula already had the Browning from her shoulder holster gripped in her lap. She twisted round, stared through the rear window.

'Thank God for Harry's armoured glass. That bullet, the starred glass is in direct line with your head.'

'I was driving slowly,' Tweed remarked calmly, 'so it wouldn't take a top marksman to aim at me.'

'You look pleased,' she snapped. 'Can't imagine why.'

'That bullet is significant. Shows we came to the right area. Someone doesn't like us poking round here. Or,' he suggested amiably, 'maybe it's Lord Bullerton's way of saying welcome to Hobart House.'

7

The high hedge to their right ended suddenly and Paula sat up. A panoramic view of great beauty opened before them. The hedge had masked a vast green bowl descending down a steep slope. Towards the rear was a single house perched on a small hill.

'I've never seen a more attractive house,' Paula commented.

'Looks to me like an original Georgian,' Tweed replied. 'Which means it's a perfect cube – the length of the front will be the same as the sides.'

'And it has a sea-blue lake in the huge space in front of it.'

'So, we have found Hobart House. I wonder what sort of a reception we'll get . . .'

He was driving down the steep curving hill as Paula studied the landscape. Some distance behind the

71

house the ground rose to a grim bleak moor covered with gorse, which appeared to be black.

A small brown Ford was parked at the foot of marble steps leading up to a wide terrace. Tweed parked behind it. As they mounted the steps the front door opened, a man walked out, the door closed behind him.

'Falkirk, of all people,' Paula whispered.

The private detective was more smartly dressed than usual. He wore a new leather jacket, a cravat at his neck, well-cut blue trousers. He stared at Paula with a hint of amusement in his alert eyes.

'What a surprise,' he remarked. 'Makes my day to see my favourite girl friend.'

'And that will be your day,' she snapped.

'I guess you must have had me followed,' he sneered. 'Must be an expert shadow. Never saw him. Enjoy yourselves,' he went on, ignoring Tweed, 'I have to get things done.'

'We'll talk later,' Tweed said grimly.

'It will be my pleasure,' Falkirk called out as he jumped athletically behind the wheel of the Ford. He drove off at a dangerous speed up the curving road, leaving a trail of dust in his wake.

'Not now,' Tweed warned as Paula opened her mouth.

He pressed the bell, then raised the polished knocker, rattled it loudly. In less than thirty seconds the door opened and a tall woman dressed in black, with a Roman nose and an unpleasant expression, stood there.

'What is it?' she demanded.

'My name is Tweed. I have to see Lord Bullerton urgently.'

'His Lordship does not see callers without an appointment.'

'I don't make appointments.' Tweed showed her his folder. 'I have to see him now. At once.'

'I'll inform him you called.'

She slammed the door in his face. Tweed paced the front, then measured the left-hand side. He thought he saw a huge shadow which immediately vanished. He returned as the front door opened again. The tall woman in black eyed Paula with disfavour.

'His Lordship has decided to make an exception in your case. The girl will remain in your car.'

'She is my chief assistant, goes everywhere with me. So she will come with me now.'

'You might have mentioned that earlier. And don't trip over the shag carpet.'

She was referring to the fact that the small panelled hall's floor was covered wall-to-wall with the carpet. Tweed felt his ankles sinking into it. She led them to a door in the right-hand wall, opened it, made her announcement.

'Mr Tweed, sir. Also the female assistant he insisted must accompany him.'

A very large man jumped with surprising agility out of an armchair, walked rapidly across to his visitors, his outsize hand extended in greeting. The head on a thick neck seemed huge. Below thick fair hair his prominent forehead suggested intelligence, beneath his thick eyebrows large blue eyes stared at each of them in turn. His nose was aggressive above a strong mouth and below that jowls were developing.

Paula was taken aback by their host's sheer size, but like many big men his feet were small and neat. His voice was powerful.

'You are so welcome, Mr Tweed. A visitor of great importance who arrived in Gunners Gorge yesterday and is staying at the Nag's Head.'

He was smiling warmly as he shook Tweed's hand and then turned to Paula to shake hers.

'I am losing my manners. I should have greeted the delightful Miss Paula Grey first. Mr Tweed's brilliant aide-de-camp.'

'Lord Bullerton?' she queried, tensing her hand, expecting it to be crushed in his great paw. Instead he squeezed gently, holding on longer than is normal.

'Yes,' he answered her, 'for my sins I am Lord Bullerton. My venerable late father insisted I carry on the line. Three of us so we shall sit round this table. The chairs are very comfortable.' He glanced at the open door where the woman who had let them in stood waiting for orders. 'Mrs Shipton, drinks all round. I'll have a neat double Scotch. Tweed?'

'The same as yourself.'

'Most important of all. Miss Grey?'

'I'd like a French Chardonnay in a small glass.'

'We only serve French,' Mrs Shipton said severely as she walked to a large glass-windowed cupboard which appeared more like a bar.

'And I see you know Mr Falkirk,' Tweed commented, settled in one of the tapestry-covered carver chairs. 'A private detective.'

Tweed doesn't waste time, Paula thought. Plunges straight in.

'Ah, Falkirk,' Bullerton sighed. 'Touts for business round the shires.'

Mrs Shipton had served the drinks, placing a large cloth mat in front of each of them before perching their drink on top of it.

'At least Mr Falkirk made an appointment,' she snapped, went into the hall, slamming the door behind her.

'*Mrs Shipton!*' thundered Bullerton.

'Sir?' she called out, reopening the door.

'Point one,' Bullerton continued thundering, 'I can do without your commentaries. Point two, when you leave this room I like the door closed quietly.'

Mrs Shipton, her expression venomous, left again, closing the door without a whisper.

'Your housekeeper?' Paula enquired.

'Shsh!' Bullerton laid a hand on hers. 'House manager.'

'You seem to have a lot of spies,' Tweed remarked. 'When we arrived you knew a lot about us.'

'Ah! Mr Tweed. You are in the country now. Anyone new and the gossip starts . . .'

'Indeed it does,' intervened Paula. 'You have five daughters and one son.'

'Yes.' Bullerton sighed. 'The two eldest, Nancy and

Petra, walked out on me. Wished to travel, I gather. Nancy went to Canada. Had just one postcard from her. Toronto. Petra pushed off to Australia. Again only one postcard – Sydney. But I still have Margot and Sable—'

As though on cue the door burst open and a wild girl burst into the room. Fair-haired, she wore baggy jeans, a short jumper which exposed a generous display of bare stomach, and Reeboks on her feet. She dropped a briefcase by a couch and hurtled over to Tweed. He held out a hand and she slapped it in a friendly gesture with her own.

'This is Margot,' Bullerton said in a resigned tone.

'I like you,' Margot said to Tweed, dragging a chair close. 'I'm so fed up with the young idiots. Just dumped a boy friend. Only one part of my anatomy he was interested in. Tried to drag me behind a bush up on Black Gorse Moor. I gave him my knee. Left him crouched over and moaning. I prefer more mature men.'

The door opened and Mrs Shipton appeared again. She seemed in a better mood now as she addressed her employer.

'Sir, that important call you expected has come through. You could take it in the library. The line is bad. I think he's using a mobile.'

Bullerton stood up, excusing himself to his guests. He wore jodhpurs tucked into gleaming boots and riding kit. The garb seemed quite normal in this part of the world. As he was leaving, a very attractive slim girl appeared. She was fashionably dressed in an expensive two-piece blue suit. Her fair hair was neatly coiffured and Paula estimated her to be in her early twenties.

'This is Sable,' Bullerton called over his shoulder before he left the drawing room.

'Oh, God!' Margot said in a loud voice.

She began running two fingers up the sleeve of Tweed's arm. Her smile was inviting when Sable spoke. She had a cultured voice and a very pleasant manner as she spoke to Margot.

'I'm not sure Mr Tweed likes you doing that during his first visit.'

'Drop dead,' Margot snapped. 'Just because you manipulated Pater into sending you to Heathfield you think you're the cat's whiskers,' she went on nastily. 'I went to a good school but it wasn't Heathfield . . .'

'Calm down, Margot,' Sable said quietly, still standing.

'You shove off,' screamed Margot. 'You weren't invited to this party!'

She jumped up, advanced on Sable, her right fist clenched ready to punch her sister in the stomach. Sable, taller, stood very still, shot out her long arms, her hands on Margot's shoulders. She gave Margot a violent shove. Margot staggered backwards, ended up sprawled in an armchair.

Sable fingered a diamond brooch attached to the top of her jacket. Margot leaned forward, screaming as she felt under the left leg of her jeans. She pulled out a knife from a holster attached to her lower leg.

'See that!' she screamed. 'Pater's birthday present to his pet, Sable.'

Margot leapt to her feet. She rushed at Sable, knife raised to slash her. Sable remained quite still. Then as Margot reached her one long arm shot out, the hand grasped Margot's knife hand by the wrist, twisted. Margot yelled in pain and dropped the knife. At that moment during the struggle Lord Bullerton returned.

'Couldn't hear a word . . . bloody hell. Margot, are you mad?'

'We had a disagreement,' Margot replied sullenly, sitting on the armchair, nursing her twisted wrist.

Tweed leaned forward, studied the knife. One side had a keen blade, the other a regular serrated edge. Not the weapon which had been used to carve up the faces of the two women in London.

A good-looking young man in his early twenties entered the room. Wearing a neat grey suit, his features were striking and his eyes almond-shaped, which gave him an air of authority.

'This is Lance, my son . . . and this is Margot again,' he said in a voice rumbling with fury.

'*Again*. Always Margot again,' Margot yelled in fury.

Bullerton raised one huge hand, slapped her so hard across the face Paula thought he would take her head off. Then he administered the same harsh blow to the other side of her face. She burst into tears and ran from the room.

'I'll get rid of this,' said Lance.

He picked up the knife by the handle, walked across to a door a distance beyond the bar, opened it and Paula saw it led to a marble-tiled toilet. He came out with a large towel wrapped round the knife.

'Plenty of deep fissures on the moor,' he explained. 'It will be safe down there. I never knew Margot went in for knives.'

'I'll give her hell later,' Bullerton growled.

'May I suggest you don't?' requested Lance. 'I'll arrange for Mrs Shipton to prepare a nice tea for her. Muffins, which Margot loves, plenty of butter, Dundee cake and a large pot of tea. I'll take it up to her myself.'

'All right. If you think that's best. You'd make a good candidate to carry on the title when I'm gone.'

'He really doesn't want that,' Sable's cultured tones broke in. 'He's told you that enough times.'

'No, he doesn't,' Bullerton agreed after Lance had left. 'I think now you'd make a better job of it. You're competent, controlled, don't mind responsibility – which Lance does. And you're popular with the people who count.'

'Let me make one thing clear,' Sable said firmly. 'I'm not asking for it or assuming anything. You do change your mind quite often.'

'True enough,' he agreed. 'But I've been thinking about the whole business.'

'Time we left,' Tweed suggested. 'It has been interesting. I think you've got the gem of a house. A real Georgian.'

'I'll come out on the terrace with you. Sable, join us, please.' As he walked out with Tweed, Mrs Shipton appeared with another double Scotch on a tray. Bullerton, standing on the terrace, drank half, licked his thick lips and swallowed the rest, dumping the glass back on the tray, which Mrs Shipton took back into the house.

'His third,' Sable whispered to Paula. 'Watch out. And could I come to see you at the Nag's Head?'

'You'd be most welcome. Best to phone me first. Here's my number . . .'

She gave the number to Sable, expecting her to record it in a notebook. Instead, Sable merely glanced at it.

'Got it,' she said and disappeared into the hall.

Paula walked towards the wall of the terrace Bullerton and Tweed were heading for. She studied the large man's walk. Perfectly steady. She joined them as Tweed posed the question.

'Why is it called Gunners Gorge?'

'Ah, sir. There's some history. In the sixteen hundreds the son of the great Cromwell was fighting with the Parliamentarians. At least, one of his generals was. Royalists were waiting near Worcester for their cavalry to come from here to smash the Parliamentarians. With me?'

'I know a little about the final battle at Worcester.'

'Well' – Bullerton's huge face was becoming red – 'spies had reported to the general that the Royalist cavalry had set a trap in the town here to destroy his cavalry. Arriving early, the ambushers took up position in the entrances to the caves near the top of the gorge. Cromwell's cavalry outwitted them.'

Bullerton was talking more rapidly, as though enjoying relating the outcome.

'That means,' Tweed speculated, 'they were looking down on the road which passes the Nag's Head.'

'Which was the road the Royalist cavalry would ride along,' said Bullerton, gleefully. 'And they did, sir!'

'What happened?'

'The Cromwellian cavalry rode straight up the stepped alleys. This gave them a commanding position overlooking the caves. Their muskets laid down a murderous barrage of fire, firing point blank into the caves.'

He rubbed his large hands together as though seeing it all with sadistic enjoyment.

'The Royalist ambushers – and their horses – were massacred on that famous day. Dead Royalists – and their horses – fell into the falls and the gorge which was running – streaming – with blood. What a sight it must have been!'

His face was now a mottled red, his eyes gleaming with delight. Paula was appalled.

She saw a green Bugatti driving slowly down the road towards Hobart House. Bullerton glared as the gleaming car parked behind Tweed's Audi.

'He's early, damn him.' Paula immediately recognized the driver.

It was Archie MacBlade, the oil prospector whose

picture had been in the newspaper. But a very different MacBlade. He'd had his hair cut, his previously bushy moustache was neatly trimmed. He wore leather driving kit. He looked handsome and she was rather taken by him as he leapt up the steps. Bullerton had turned his back on him, was slowly stomping towards the house.

MacBlade was smiling as he approached Tweed and Paula, holding out his hand. Bullerton looked round, saw the gesture and shouted at the top of his voice.

'Don't start jabbering to them. They're only guests. Come in *now*!'

'I'm coming,' MacBlade called back. A pause. 'When I am ready.

'I am so pleased to meet you,' he went on, 'Mr Tweed and Miss Paula Grey. Such a distinguished couple, if I may say so.'

'You may say so,' Paula replied with a warm smile. 'And both of us appreciate your generous compliment.'

'In that case,' MacBlade suggested, 'may I invite you both to be my guests for dinner in the Silver Room one evening?'

'That would suit us perfectly. We look forward to enjoying the company of the most professional oil prospector in the world.'

'Once.' MacBlade smiled again. 'I am now retired.'

'Really?'

Paula thought she detected a note of scepticism in Tweed's tone. At that moment there was a frustrated roar from Bullerton, waiting by the door.

'Don't make the mistake of thinking he is drunk,' MacBlade warned just before he left them. 'His capacity for absorbing liquor is limitless. He is just play-acting . . .'

Paula pursed her lips as she watched MacBlade walk casually to the house.

'We have just seen the real Pit Bull,' she said grimly.

8

'I'd like to go for a walk on the moor,' Paula decided, 'to get that horror story Bullerton revelled in out of my mind. There are more steps at the end of the terrace.'

'I'll come with you,' said Tweed. 'There's stony ground higher up. I'll get our motoring gloves out of the car. Then if we trip up we won't rip our hands . . .'

They walked a long way across recently trimmed grass, then the slope began. So did the rough ground, littered with stones of different colours. Paula, wearing her gloves, reached the edge of the moor first. Behind her, Tweed, who had a very sensitive nose for odours, pulled a face.

Paula eased her way along a narrow path between tall gorse bushes with blackened stems. There were few yellow blooms and even they were drooping. There was something unpleasant about the atmosphere.

'Not like the Yorkshire moors,' Tweed commented.

He used his gloved hand to grasp a handful of gorse, raised it to his nose. The gorse had a greasy feel. They pushed on through the winding path until they reached the top. Along a flat stretch ran a narrow-gauge railway.

'What's this?' Paula asked.

She had bent down to where the last gorse bushes enclosed the path on both sides. She hauled out a long thick steel rod with a wide flat steel top. Tweed peered over her shoulder.

'That,' he told her, 'is like the pillars they once used in coal mines to support the roofs in deep tunnels. And beyond that little railway there are deep runnels in the ground – as though made by heavy trucks.'

'That nauseous smell. What is it?' she wondered.

'Probably from an industrial plant beyond the ridge over there. Belching out pollution, which it shouldn't.'

'I don't like this place. It's creepy.'

Tweed didn't hear her. He was returning downhill along the path at an incredible rate. She followed slowly, watching her footing. Near the bottom of the path she noticed dead gorse piled up in a large heap. Bending down, she carefully removed the branches and foliage. Reaching the ground level she stared.

She had exposed the entrance to a large tunnel. It comprised a new steel pipe at least three feet in diameter. Taking out a torch, she shone it into the tunnel, which gradually went lower and lower. The metal was perfectly clean.

She rearranged the concealing gorse over the entrance. As she stood up she noticed a large boulder near the end of the path. A marker?

Tweed was far below, heading for Hobart House. The moment she reached the grass her legs flew to catch him up. Out of breath, she arrived to find him standing at the Audi. She was on the verge of mentioning the tunnel when she saw his absorbed expression.

They were driving back up the curving road when she looked back to catch a glimpse of the beauty of the Georgian house. It had the outward appearance of a dream house.

'I sensed deceit and evil inside that house,' she mused.

'They do say that the family can be the bloodiest battlefield,' he replied as though his mind was on something else.

'I noticed that Sable decided not to come out onto the terrace. I suspect she sensed her father's change of mood.'

'Possibly. The strange thing is this case started out with the bestial murder of two women in London. Which is why we came up here. Now I wonder.'

'You wonder what?'

'I'm not being fanciful. You know that's not my style. Now I really do wonder.'

'Wonder what?' she persisted.

'We may by chance have walked in on something which is bigger, much bigger than I ever foresaw.'

9

They were driving slowly along the hedge-lined lane leading to the Village when Paula glanced at the slim leather executive case Tweed had taken into Hobart House but had never opened.

'That wouldn't contain those photos Hector gave you – the pics of the two murdered women looking normal?'

'It does.'

'I'm surprised you didn't show them to Lord Bullerton.'

'Not when Sable and Margot were about.'

'What did you think of Margot? Bit of a wild cat.'

'Sisters often dislike, even hate each other. I thought that Sable was being provocative, the way she fingered her diamond brooch when she came into the drawing room.'

'I rather liked Sable.'

'Maybe,' he replied, 'but you know your own gender.'

'I also thought it odd when Falkirk turned up. Looking for a job? Could it be his host covered him by giving that as a reason? I'm wondering who *has* hired Falkirk.'

'A number of candidates. Lord Bullerton, Chief Inspector Reedbeck or Archie MacBlade, to name just some prospects . . . Look in front. I don't believe it.'

A battered grey Fiat had shot out from a gap in the hedge in front of them. Harry Butler, at the wheel, waved to them as he drove at their pace into the Village High Street, turning right towards Gunners Gorge.

'Now where has Harry been the past few hours?' Paula mused.

'I expect he'll tell us.' They had entered Gunners Gorge and Harry drove under the arch leading to the car park of the Nag's Head. 'He may have information from London . . .'

Parked in one corner was a new Maserati. Harry pointed to it as they stood next to their vehicles.

'That means Lance Mandeville is floating around somewhere – Bullerton's twenty-year-old athletic son. Polite, I gather he is popular in town. I've got something for you, Tweed. It came by courier. I persuaded him to give it to me by showing him my identity folder.'

Tweed broke the seal on the envelope Harry handed him. A brief note from Howard, then a large document on hand-made paper. He scanned it quickly, then passed it to Paula.

'Professor Saafeld's preliminary autopsy report. Now we know how those two women were slaughtered.'

'Do we?' Paula asked after reading the document Tweed had handed to her. 'Chloroform?'

'Saafeld found traces of it in the nostrils and mouth of the woman murdered in the house next to Lisa Clancy's – but none on the other woman, who was murdered in the house round the corner. The killer had reconnoitred the area earlier. He'd seen the second victim took a lot of time making that lock on her door work. He attacks the other one first by pressing a pad soaked with chloroform over her nose and mouth. He then cuts her throat, ruins her face. Darting round the corner, he finds his second target trying to get her key to work, comes up behind her, swiftly hauls back her long hair, uses his knife.'

'I must be thick. You're right . . .' Paula still had half her mind on the tunnel she'd discovered on Black Gorse Moor, something she still hadn't mentioned to Tweed.

'More news,' Harry reported tersely. 'I know who fired the bullet at you on your way to Hobart House. Lepard.'

'So a lot of money is changing hands among the killer thugs,' Tweed commented. 'Which means we're looking for someone with wealth . . .'

'And you are the target,' Harry warned. 'Lepard

fired from behind a hedge. I was close behind in my car. I drove straight through a gap to get him. He was too quick – sped off aboard a Harley-Davidson.'

'How can you be sure it was Lepard?' Tweed demanded.

'He's half-French, half-British, as I explained. Bob Newman was an ace international reporter and he's still very good at description. Lepard is slim, clean-shaven, with a sallow complexion. I know it was him because he turned to look at me before vanishing over a slope. News gets worse.'

'That's right, Harry,' Paula joked, 'cheer us up . . .'

'Newman has been back to check with his East End informant. All the killer thugs have been put on instant standby. My guess is they'll be up here any day – after Lepard failed to get you.'

'Then call Bob and tell him I want the whole team ready to come up here pretty damn fast.'

'Consider it done.'

Harry dived back into his car, drove slowly out under the arch.

'I was right,' said Tweed as they walked back into the hotel. 'And someone up here is reporting our every move. We have stumbled into something *very* big.'

The landlord, Bowling, was not behind his reception counter, which was unusual. Paula spotted a guest perched on a sofa, studying some kind of chart. He folded it quickly and stood up. Archie MacBlade.

'We're starting to bump into each other,' he said with a warm smile. 'For me that is a pleasure.'

'Do you often visit Gunners Gorge?' she asked casually.

'Occasionally. It is quiet and gets me away from the world.' He turned to Tweed with an unusual expression in his eyes. 'You have an enigmatic visitor waiting to see you in the lounge. A Lance Mandeville, son of Lord Bullerton.'

'Mandeville?'

'That's the family name.' He glanced round the reception area, checking that they were alone, then produced a business card, scribbled a name on the back, tucked it inside Tweed's top pocket. 'That's a tip you might like to follow up. Mr Hartland Trent. Has a sense of humour – lives at Twinkle Cottage, Primrose Steps. Turn right when you leave the hotel. The flights of steps instead of roads climb the hill. He's halfway up the third flight. Must go now.'

'One second,' Tweed said quickly. 'What does Trent do?'

'Landowner and astute businessman. The only trustworthy man in the Gorge. Really must fly . . .'

'I don't think he likes Lance,' Paula whispered. 'Did you see his expression when he stared directly at you?'

'Not a question of liking would be my interpretation of the odd expression.'

'Well, come on,' she urged, squeezing his arm. 'So what would be your interpretation?'

'More like a warning.'

10

They descended the steps into the hotel lounge. Tables were laid for tea. In a corner, Lance stood up from a table to greet them, his slim hand extended. He pulled out a chair for Paula, who took off her leather jacket.

'May I?' suggested Lance, taking the jacket to hang from the back of her chair. 'I am so glad you could join me,' he said to Tweed. 'They have excellent muffins here. I hope you are both hungry.'

'Ravenous,' replied Tweed as Lance sat opposite Paula. 'I could tackle all those.'

A smartly dressed waitress had placed a large metal container on the table, carefully removed the top without the flourish used in London restaurants. They began eating, Tweed scooping up large quantities of strawberry jam, ignoring the small talk between Lance and Paula.

Paula was studying Lance. He was clad in a smart blue blazer with gold buttons, a Liberty cravat at his neck, his black hair neatly brushed. She was impressed by his good manners, his handsome face; fascinated by his almond-shaped eyes.

'I really come here as an emissary from my father,' Lance began.

'Oh, really,' Tweed responded in a bored tone as he drank tea the waitress had served from Wedgwood china.

'He wishes me to pass his unreserved apologies to both of you for his behaviour when you were leaving . . .'

'Does he?' commented Tweed, now busy consuming the first of two large apple tarts garnished with cream, his eye on the massive Dundee cake in the middle of the table.

'When his other visitor had left—'

'Archie MacBlade in his Bugatti,' Tweed remarked.

'Oh, you know him?' Lance enquired sharply.

'Saw his picture in the paper,' Tweed said as he cut a huge slice of Dundee cake.

'My father would regard it as an honour if you dined with him at Hobart House this evening,' continued Lance in his uphill conversational struggle with Tweed, smiling all the time.

'My father wasn't drunk,' Lance pressed on. 'He can consume a large quantity without it affecting him. Reminds me of what I read in a Winston Churchill biography. Winston once said he'd taken more out of alcohol than alcohol had taken out of him.'

'Do your sisters Sable and Margot like each other?' Tweed asked suddenly.

'I'm afraid they hate each other . . .'

'*Why?*' Tweed demanded.

'Sable is my father's favourite. She'd like to be Lady Bullerton when he passes away one day.'

'Peculiar,' Tweed said, having finished his cake. 'Normally the title descends to a male relative. In this case yourself.'

'I don't want the damned title. Excuse me,' he said to Paula. 'All that responsibility. I prefer to enjoy myself. As to tradition, when King John, or whoever it was, conferred the title on an ancestor centuries ago, a special clause was added that if a male candidate refused to accept it then the title passed to the nearest female available.'

'And in this case Sable?' Tweed suggested.

'It would actually be Margot, who was born a year before Sable.'

'And yet Sable is your father's favourite. Why?'

'He thinks her personality is superior to Margot's, gives her fantastically expensive presents on her birthday.'

'Like the diamond brooch she flaunted,' Tweed said grimly.

'Flaunted?'

For the first time the smile vanished off Lance's face, was replaced by a sneering curl of his lips.

'Never mind,' said Tweed.

'I expect you have a lot of girl friends,' Paula intervened, appalled by Tweed's aggressive treatment of everything Lance had said.

'Oh, lots and lots,' Lance said, the smile returning when he turned to her. 'I'm afraid I'm rather wicked. I've got a small pad in Gunners Gorge Father doesn't know about. When a girl attracts my attention I settle her there. Until she starts talking about marriage. Then I wait until she's out. I pack all her things neatly in her suitcase, place it in the hall, get the locks changed at once.'

'Isn't that a bit tough on her?' Paula suggested.

'Until she gets home,' Lance said with a grin. 'When she unpacks she finds an envelope stuffed with money.'

'That probably eases her sorrow,' Paula said with a smile.

'Don't much care whether it does or not. Self-interest is what drives the world.' He turned to Tweed, tried again. 'Would it be possible for the two of you to dine with my father at Hobart House this evening?'

'Don't see why not. What time?'

'Would 8 p.m. suit you, sir?'

'Yes, it would.' Tweed stood up, abruptly the soul of good humour. 'Please thank your father and say we're looking forward to seeing him again. Also, I would like to thank you for the truly excellent tea. To get this in London you'd have to go to the Ritz or the Savoy. I have enjoyed every minute of it. Thank you. Please excuse us – we must leave now . . .'

★

'I think you were pretty tough on Lance,' Paula commented as they walked through the entrance hall, keeping her voice low.

'You've certainly been with me long enough to know I adapt my tactics to obtain information. They worked.'

'It's been raining while we were having tea,' Paula remarked, gazing through the front entrance before Tweed turned into the garage.

'Buckets of it,' called out landlord Bowling. 'All the time you were having tea. Drenched down – a cloudburst. The river has risen. It will be coming over the falls like an express train.'

'What did you think of Lance?' Tweed asked as they entered the garage and headed for his Audi.

'Very smooth. Too smooth for my liking. I would never trust him despite his good looks – which he obviously exploits to the full.'

'I think, like the others round here, with the exception of old Mrs Grout, he was lying. Now I want to drive all the way along the High Street and up to Aaron's Rock at the top of the gorge. Should be quite a sight after all the rain . . .'

As he was cruising along the High Street, Paula used her binoculars to study the road on the far side of the river. On each bank a wide area of grass separated road from river.

'They call that road on the far side Ascot Way,' she observed. 'The horsy lot must live over there. Tweed, could you park for a moment? I've spotted the path which probably leads to the stone Pit Bull had erected when Lizbeth drowned.'

'*If* she drowned,' Tweed said as he climbed out, following Paula along the curving path through lush green grass.

'Why "if"?' Paula called back.

'They found her clothes neatly piled by the river. Despite the fact everyone agrees she was sloppy and untidy in her habits. The discrepancy bothers me.'

'Look at the wording on the stone,' she exclaimed.

FOR LIZBETH
YOU WILL RETURN ONE DAY
YOUR LOVING FATHER

'It doesn't add up,' she protested. 'The affection. When you think this is the same man who stormed off the terrace as we were leaving. How abusive he was – not only to us but also to Archie MacBlade.'

'I agree. We still don't know what sort of a man Lord Bullerton really is. As I've told you before, human nature is a fascinating and complex mixture. Now for the Gorge. The river is indeed very high.'

Lepard sat in a chair overlooking the High Street closer to the Gorge. He had chosen the only accommodation available for a two-week stay, a cottage with a notice in the front window. *Room Available For short Let.*

He would never be recognized now even in the East End. He wore a large grey shaggy wig with a very British wide-brimmed straw hat he never took off. He had explained to his landlady, Mrs Wharton, that he had been ill, that the doctor had warned him never to expose his head to the sun and to protect his hands. He therefore always wore gloves. No fingerprints. He had even gone to the lengths of wearing contact lenses that changed the colour of his eyes. To complete the disguise he now wore large horn-rimmed spectacles with plain glass. With his disguise removed he was confident Mrs Wharton would never pick him out of a police line up, if it ever came to that.

On his mobile he told his second-in-command, Ned Marsh, to bring up a bazooka with rockets when he summoned his gang to Gunners Gorge.

He had foreseen that Tweed might summon his key team. In which case it would be a massacre, probably launched by his gang from the top of the Gorge, which he had explored very thoroughly. The window he watched through was masked by dense net curtains. He could see out but no one could see in. The only disadvantage was he was too far up the High Street to view the Gorge or its summit.

He sat up straight with shock as Tweed's Audi cruised slowly past. If it was Tweed's habit to travel the same route he was a dead man.

'You know,' said Paula as they neared the turn-off

leading direct to the summit of the Gorge, 'I don't see how Cromwell's cavalry ever climbed those steps as Bullerton described. Hooves would slither all over them.'

'You've missed something,' he told her. 'Alongside each flight there is a wide grass verge between steps and the beautiful houses. Horses could easily mount as high as they needed to by galloping up the grass.'

'Of course. I missed that,' she admitted.

'Another thing,' he went on. 'Last night before I got into bed I phoned Marler and asked him to come up here today, so he could arrive at any moment.'

'Why Marler?' she wondered.

'Because he is a master strategist. So it's important that he checks the lie of the land, especially in this area.'

Further down the High Street, Lepard was still watching through the net curtains, seated comfortably in his chair behind a table. A few minutes after spotting Tweed's Audi he saw the next vehicle, a green Saab, driving slowly towards the Gorge. Without passengers there was a single driver behind the wheel. Lepard saw no significance in this brief event, assuming it was one of the locals . . .

Approaching the turn-off to Aaron's Rock, Paula became aware of a disturbing sound, a muted roar of great power which steadily increased as Tweed drove up a steep dusty track. On either side high granite boulders gave her a feeling of claustrophobia.

They were in the open now. Tweed turned the Audi

round for a swift departure. Jumping out of his car he was followed more slowly by Paula. She was staring at a huge cloud of spray and the roar had become deafening.

Determined to keep up with Tweed she ran after and past him, stopping suddenly as she gazed at the awesome spectacle. The river was the kind of surge you see when a massive dam breaks. Her feet and her willpower carried her towards the brink and she stared down.

The immense rush of water, culminating in the huge waterfall dropping a hundred and fifty feet, hypnotized her. She began to feel dizzy as her feet took her two more steps over the wet, slippery surface of the platform of rock projecting over endless space. She thought she heard Tweed shout but the thunder of the waterfall drowned him out.

The next thing she knew he had one strong arm round her waist, the other gripping her arm tightly. He put his mouth close to her ear.

'You idiot! You will now do exactly what I tell you. I want you to slowly back away. *Slow* steps. This platform is like a skating rink. Do *not* attempt to turn round. One foot at a time. That is an order!'

She obeyed. She had the strange sensation Tweed had lifted her off her feet. He hadn't. Her right boot slipped as she was moving it back. She was terrified. She was going to slide over the edge. Tweed's arm tightened round her waist until she felt she could hardly breathe, her face running with spray as an exceptional surge of water arrived from higher up the river. Tweed's voice was in her ear again.

'Nearly off the platform,' he said gently. 'Just a few more steps and we're there. Then you can cry all you like . . .'

'I'm not crying,' she shouted, furious. 'It's spray off the waterfall!'

Her burst of indignation seemed to give her new strength. A few more steps and she'd be clear of this hideous platform. Her right ankle sank into the sand at the top of the road. She gave a great sigh of relief.

'You did very well,' a familiar voice drawled. 'Sit down on this armchair.' Marler had spread out a waterproof sheet on a flatstone. 'And have a drink,' he went on as he offered her an uncapped flask.

'Is that alcohol?' she asked cautiously.

'No, you little boozer,' he told her, raising his voice. 'It is water. You go first. And leave a generous portion for Tweed and me . . .'

She thanked him, comfortably seated, began sipping slowly, feeling much better. Marler, who had foreseen conditions, wore a raincoat, a small camera with a zoom lens slung from his neck.

'You've got nerve,' Marler told Paula.

'I was scared witlesss . . .'

'So was Tweed. So will I be, on that platform.'

'What are you going to do?' Tweed asked.

'See what is on the other side of this gorge?'

Neither of them had noticed until Marler pointed. On the far side of the Gorge three large caves had been at some time carved out of the rock at their level, two more at the level below. Paula noticed they were high enough to accommodate men on horseback, recalling Bullerton's vivid description of the battle long ago.

'Lepard,' Marler explained, 'will, I am confident, station his killers inside them. They overlook the road, or the first part of it. Tweed, do you often drive your Audi along that road?'

'I was thinking of doing so each morning . . .'

'Good. So you will be the target.'

'Oh, no!' protested Paula.

'Please keep quiet, dear, until I'm finished,' admonished Marler. 'It won't be Tweed driving, it will be a member of the team clothed to look like Tweed. Probably have to draw lots for the driver, since they'll all volunteer.'

'Not necessary,' Tweed insisted in a strong voice. 'Because I *will* be behind the wheel.'

'In that case I will be with you,' snapped Paula.

'No, you won't. And that is another order,' Tweed said, as he stared at her grimly.

'Time to take my pics of those caves so I can show the team.'

'You'd better be very careful of that platform,' Paula warned.

'I'll be OK. Look . . .'

He lifted a foot and he was wearing rubber gumboots; the soles had rubber projections which would increase balance. He waved a hand, walked to the platform, stamped a foot on its surface and marched across as though on grass. He went to the edge, took a lot of pics of the caves at both levels, returned smiling.

'Back to the Nag's Head,' he suggested. 'I've booked a room in my name. Also I've booked rooms for the rest of the team, telling the landlord, Bowling, they are members of the Fishers' Club. I've further instructed Bob Newman to include among the more lethal equipment fishing rods and tackle. They're waiting now for your signal to hurtle up here.'

'Excellent organization. What I don't know is where the team will be located to counter Lepard's thugs.'

'Another leaf out of the Cromwellian book. They will occupy positions up a series of three flights of steps to our right as we drive back to the hotel. Most residences I found were empty. These wealthy people take early holidays.'

'Let's get back, then,' Tweed suggested, walking towards Marler's Saab, parked next to Tweed's Audi.

'One vital factor you should be warned about. Newman found out that one of Lepard's men is bringing him a bazooka. One round from that hitting your Audi and, despite armoured plate and armoured glass, your vehicle will go up in flames.'

'This is not on,' Paula said vehemently just before they climbed into their transport.

'Our team,' Marler assured her, 'scattered along those steps, have a clear view of all the caves. It will be up to me to spot the man with the bazooka and before the team opens fire to kill him stone cold dead.'

'It's too much of a risk to Tweed,' she snapped.

'All our previous operations have involved risk,' Tweed said.

'Not as suicidal as this one,' she snapped again.

'Marler,' suggested Tweed, to change the subject, 'I think it would be wiser if we were not seen together. Maybe you could drive back to the Nag's Head now and we'll start in just a few minutes.'

'All great minds,' Marler said cheerfully. 'I was just about to suggest the same thing myself. And whenever our team is summoned urgently from Park Crescent by you I shan't say one word . . .'

They had waited five minutes for Marler to get clear. Paula was staring upriver. The whole of that area north of Gunners Gorge had been obscured by mist. Now a breeze had dispersed it and she could see a long way. She tugged Tweed's sleeve.

'Look at that. An old iron bridge. It must link Ascot Way with the High Street. I did see a girl riding a horse heading up Ascot Way. I wondered how she'd reach the hunting country on our side.'

'Now you know,' he said without interest as they climbed in into the Audi. Tweed began driving down the track, turning right as they entered the High Street.

'Why did you send Marler off ahead of us?' she began. 'I've the odd suspicion you had another motive.'

'Can't keep anything from you.' He sighed. 'You are right. Remember that business card Archie MacBlade tucked into my pocket in the hall of the Nag's Head?'

'I do.'

'He urged me to visit a Mr Hartland Trent. Said he was trustworthy. Trent could be just the man to tell us what is really going on in this strange town.'

11

Tweed parked the Audi several flights below Primrose Steps. No point in advertising who he was going to visit. He ran up the flight with Paula by his side. He realized all the expensive, well-designed houses were built of grim dark grey granite.

Twinkle Cottage was high up the flight, more than halfway. He hammered twice with the large brass knocker. The heavy door swung inward. He glanced at Paula, who already had her Browning in her hand. He slipped out his own weapon, pushed open the well-oiled door.

He did not call out as so often happens in films. Anyone might be waiting inside. He walked slowly in on the wall-to-wall carpet. He listened. No sound of anyone. With Paula close behind him he continued until he reached a partly opened door on his right. He pushed it open a little more into a spacious living room.

'My God!' he said under his breath.

'What is it?' whispered Paula, who had acute hearing.

'I think we have found Mr Hartland Trent . . .'

The body was full length on a table whose green baize was covered with blood. Tweed gently felt a neck artery, shook his head. He then felt the face and shoulder.

'No good,' he said to Paula. 'He's dead. But the warmth of the body suggests the murder was committed not so long before we arrived. At a quick count he was stabbed brutally over a dozen times.'

'Look at the right hand, at the index finger. It's pointing at something. That pile of old newspapers on the coffee table.'

'You're not suggesting,' Tweed said in disbelief, 'that this poor devil, after being stabbed so many times, was able to turn his hand and use his finger to point.'

'We've encountered stranger cases,' she reminded him. 'Were any of the stab wounds lethal?'

'Well, no,' Tweed admitted. 'It was the loss of blood which got him. And look at the state of this room.'

It had been ransacked. Drawers were pulled out, dropped on the carpet. Bound books had been hauled out of the cases lining the walls. Paula moved suddenly,

Browning in her hand. She rushed out of the room and up a staircase.

Tweed swore to himself at his own slackness. Pulling on latex gloves, he began checking the rest of the downstairs rooms. He returned to the study as Paula dashed back down the stairs and joined him.

'I thought it was just possible the killer was still in the house,' she explained. 'Nothing. Nobody. No sign of any hurried search.'

'I should have thought of that myself earlier. I've checked downstairs. The kitchen door is locked and bolted on the inside. You know what that means?'

'Mr Hartland Trent must have known his murderer, have seen no reason to be on his guard.'

'Why is he stretched out on that table?'

'My guess is he was standing by the end of it when he was attacked. His killer pushed him onto the table and Trent tried to escape by hauling himself along it. His killer ran down the side of the table, pushed his victim down and stabbed and stabbed.'

Paula was only half-listening as she carefully opened each folded newspaper to every page. Tweed thought she was wasting her time but kept quiet, checking his watch. After a while Tweed stood up, left the room. Something had occurred to him. If someone arrived at the front door as Paula fooled around with a stack of old newspapers they would need an escape route. In the kitchen he drew back the bolts on the door. He left it locked with the key in. Just in case someone tried to get in that way.

Paula was more than halfway down the stack when he returned. After checking every page of a newspaper she folded it, perched it neatly on one side. Tweed's patience snapped.

'We must get out of this place. We need to report Hartland Trent's murder anonymously from a public phone.'

'Shut up!' she told him. 'This whole room was ransacked and the only item untouched was this pile of newspapers.' She was turning over the pages of an old copy of *The Times*. This newspaper seemed strangely thick. She reached the centre spread and stared down at a legal document and one brief typed letter on Hobart House stationery, dated five days earlier, addressed to Hartland Trent, signed by Lord Bullerton.

She scanned the document quickly, then handed it over to Tweed. It confirmed that Trent's seventy per cent holding in Black Gorse Moor would, for the sum of twenty thousand pounds, be handed over to Lord Bullerton. A note reminded Trent that the previous offer had been for seven thousand pounds.

'Do you find a phrase in clause three strange?' she asked. 'Also the wording after the line for the third signature? And I'm sure it was Trent who scrawled "refused" across the whole document.'

'I do find that phrase odd, "and all geological material". Plus the fact there are three lines at the bottom for signatures. The first presumably for Trent's, the second for Lord Bullerton's. It is the third line I find intriguing, even menacing. I don't like the wording after the third space.'

'"Sole administrator and owner of the property." So who is that?'

'At a guess, Neville Guile. I think he's concealing something, maybe his identity, behind Lord Bullerton, who is acting as his front man. Now, we must get out of here and find a public phone so you can anonymously report the murder . . .'

They left the house cautiously. Tweed had slipped the items Paula had found inside a separate compartment of the executive folder he was now carrying everywhere. Another compartment contained the photos of the two murdered women in London.

Still wearing latex gloves, he opened the door slowly, peered everywhere. No one in sight. Paula had produced a duster to rub the brass knocker which might show fingerprints Tweed had left when he'd hammered on it as they arrived.

Leaving the house, Tweed was careful to leave the front door slightly open, as they had found it earlier. As they strolled casually down the long flight, Paula slipped her arm inside Tweed's. If seen from a neighbouring house they would look like visitors.

They walked back to the parked Audi. Tweed was about to drive off when Paula produced a folded sheet from her inside pocket. She handed it to Tweed.

'This was underneath the document I found in the newspaper. You were anxious to leave so I kept it.'

The sheet of paper was a printed letterhead with Twinkle Cottage's name and address. The note, scrawled by Trent, was brief and addressed to Lord Bullerton.

You might like to know I have already sent my daughter abroad to a safe refuge. Maybe your partner would like to know this.

At the bottom was Hartland Trent's scrawled signature. Tweed handed it back to Paula, his expression grim.

'I find that grim. Clearly he was never able to post it. I now believe we are up against the most bestial villain I have so far encountered. So we won't be very choosy in the methods we use to destroy him.'

Tweed was about to turn the ignition key when they saw Harry running up the road towards them. Tweed lowered his window.

'Where's your car?' he asked.

'Out of sight in the garage. There's been a development you need to know about earliest.'

'Which is?'

'Neville Guile has arrived in town. I've been watching Hobart House from my car parked in a hole in that hedge. With field glasses. Heavily disguised. Saw him leave Hobart House and Bullerton waved him off. He could have been hidden away inside that house. I took a chance, drove back and parked in the village at this end. When Guile emerged he drove straight to the Nag's Head, booked himself a suite. Twenty-seven.'

'If he's heavily disguised how do you know it was Guile?' Tweed asked sceptically.

'Checked the register after he'd gone upstairs and the landlord had disappeared into his back room. Guile signed in with his real name.'

'How is he disguised?' Paula wondered.

'No Rolls-Royce. No chauffeur. Drives a large grey Citroën – wears a check sports suit and tinted horn-rim glasses. Has a peculiar slithery walk. While watching from the hedge I noticed on the far side of the London bowl a cottage roof with a tilting brick chimney. Place is hidden inside a copse. Guile might have stayed there to keep out of sight.'

While he waited, Paula thought, for Trent's signed contract to arrive.

'What is the position with that gang waiting in the East End?' Tweed asked.

'I checked that with Bob Newman. The gang is still scattered round the East End, except for two who have disappeared.'

'Any idea of their identities?'

'One of them I've met in a pub. A brutal piece of work. His appearance tells you. Ned Marsh. Small, powerfully built, has a crooked nose and a harelip. He's here now.'

'Here where?' Tweed pressed.

'Coming out of the garage I saw him slip furtively into the Nag's Head. Reception desk was empty. He scarpers up the stairs, vanishes. I checked the register. He hasn't booked in.'

'The pace is quickening . . .'

Briefly Tweed told Harry about their discovery of Hartland Trent. 'Maybe it was this Ned Marsh.'

'Doubt it. He's known to be a violent man but so far he's not been mixed up in a murder. I have a present for you.' Harry handed Tweed a small black instrument which reminded her of a miniature mobile phone. 'This could come in useful,' he explained. 'Latest development of a flasher by the boys down in the basement at Park Crescent. You want absolute privacy – you swivel this end round a room. This red light comes on and you've detected a hidden microphone. Press this button, a green light comes on. A radio wave wipes the bug out. Check the whole room. That's the most sophisticated device in the world.'

'Thank you, Harry. You had better leave separately. We don't want people to see us together.'

'Just about to suggest the same thing. Oh, one more thing. I saw our old friend Falkirk, the private detective. He's been away somewhere a lot. Now has a room at the Nag's Head . . .'

'I wondered what he'd do,' Tweed mused. 'After all, he was the lead who, unknown to him, brought us up to Hobartshire.'

'He won't talk,' Paula surmised.

'Yes, he will this time,' Tweed said as he drove slowly back. 'He'll tell me everything,' he said grimly, 'because of the pressure I'll put on him.'

'Then I'll leave you alone with him.'
'The eagles gather.'

Earlier, returning from the falls, they cruised past a window behind which a man sat at a table gazing through the thick net curtains. Lepard wished he had a drink to celebrate.

Driving along the target road had obviously become Tweed's favourite outing. Lepard decided he would personally aim the bazooka, the rocket with which Tweed and his Audi would be destroyed in an inferno of flames and disintegrating metal. He could hardly wait for the spectacle.

12

When they entered the hall of the hotel, Tweed glanced up the stairs. Falkirk was about to descend. Tweed held up his hand and Falkirk waited, out of sight of the visitor seated on the hall couch. Following him in, Paula saw the figure on the couch. Lance Mandeville.

He jumped up, held out his hand, squeezed hers. Always smartly clad, this time he wore a white suit: white trousers, white jacket, the collar of his white shirt open at the neck. His ensemble was completed with white shoes with gleaming brown toecaps. Reluctantly Paula admitted to herself he was very impressive.

'I've been waiting for you for ages,' he began.

'Then you've had a nice long rest.'

'I've got a proposition. Let's sit down for a minute.'

Since there was nowhere else, she joined him on the couch. He immediately moved closer to her. His almond-shaped eyes held hers lovingly. They disturbed her because she had trouble reading what was behind them.

'I have spent a certain amount of time rejecting propositions,' she told him coldly.

'Oh, God!' He slapped a hand to his forehead. 'Wrong word. I apologize. I want to ask you to have dinner with me tonight, while Mr Tweed is at Hobart House with my father. At Marcantonio's. It's a very exclusive club further up the High Street. Do you fancy caviar and champagne?'

He put his arm round her waist, exerting all his charm. She had to admit to herself he knew how to use it. She turned to look straight at him.

'Do you mind not manhandling me? Remove your arm immediately. And I do not like champagne or caviar. So forget the whole idea and shove off, please.'

His whole personality underwent a change. He jerked away his arm. The smile vanished, replaced by a sneer, his mouth twisted venomously as he jumped up.

'Women don't talk to me like that. I am Lord Bullerton's son.'

'Then go and find one who is not fussy and spends her time with you in your secret flat – until you pack her bags and throw her out.'

As he stormed out into the street Paula stood up

and the landlord appeared behind the recently deserted counter. Greeting her politely, he leaned forward to speak quietly.

'There's a gentleman waiting to see you in the drawing room.'

Paula was curious. Her first thought was it might be Archie MacBlade. She opened the door, stepped in confidently, closed the door. Stopped abruptly.

Someone had used one of the dimmer switches scattered round the walls: the room was in semi-darkness. She moved away from the door, where she would be less visible. All the lights were turned up. A man moved towards her, the only occupant in the room. Neville Guile.

Suppressing her instinct to dash back into the hall, she chose an armchair, sat very erect as he moved slowly towards her. His motion reminded her of Harry's description: he slithered to the armchair.

He no longer wore his disguise. He was dressed in a black suit. Black trousers, a long black jacket, black tie over a white shirt. He was very tall and thin and the black stressed his bloodless cadaverous face, his thin lips curved in a peculiar smile.

Paula had her hands tucked in her jacket pockets as he came close, his hand extended to shake hers. She remained still as a statue.

'You don't often get the chance to shake hands with a billionaire,' he said.

She recalled the cut-glass voice from the few words she'd heard distantly in Finden Square. She couldn't be rude. She took her right hand out of her pocket, grasped his. It was like shaking hands with a fish and he had an unpleasant way of grasping her, sliding his fingers up between hers. Without a smile she freed her hand and waited.

'I am looking for a personal assistant, Miss Grey. I know your universal reputation for incredible efficiency.' Pausing, he dabbed at his lips with a silk handkerchief. 'I would be most happy to pay you eighty thousand a year, plus benefits.'

'Thank you for the offer,' she said quickly, 'but I do have a position I totally enjoy.'

'Just so long as you have Tweed. He could be shot any day.'

'It has been tried before and he is good at surviving.'

'I have never been turned down before.' The cut-glass voice was even sharper, almost with a note of menace.

'There's always a first time.' She laughed gently. 'Might do your ego good.'

'I do wish you had not added that last sentence.' He placed his hands on his knees, prior to standing up. 'Few people have risked insulting me,' he remarked, standing up. 'And I'm not sure they're all still walking the planet . . .'

On this note his tall dark figure strode to the door. He opened it, disappeared, closed it softly.

Paula heaved a deep breath, decided she needed a long hot bath to wash off his touch.

*

After her bath Paula found her mind very alert. She assumed it was the result of the unwanted approaches she'd experienced. She was also intrigued by the hidden tunnel on Black Gorse Moor. What was going on up there?

She dressed, wearing two leather jackets, ankle boots. In her backpack she put certain items. She scribbled a note to Tweed, hoping he'd excuse her for not attending the Bullerton dinner but she felt she could sleep the evening and the night through. She wrote his name on an envelope, sealed it. She knew he'd be furious if he knew what she had decided to do.

Walking down the corridor, she paused outside Tweed's suite, pressed her ear against the door. She couldn't hear what was being said but was surprised to gather the conversation was friendly.

In the hall the landlord was absorbed explaining a map to an elegantly dressed woman. Unseen, Paula descended into the garage. No one about, thank heaven. She climbed behind the wheel of the Audi, using her own key. It was only when she emerged into the street that it occurred to her she might be driving into danger.

It was dusk when she parked the Audi in a deep hole in the hedge. She walked into the top of the bowl and saw Hobart House, far below, a blaze of lights. Getting ready for the dinner. She was relieved to see the curtains were closed.

Striding briskly, she descended the slope of the bowl, crossed it well away from the house, began to climb steeply. She sat down for a minute, took out a tough pair of jeans, hauled them on over her daytime pair. She thought she heard a noise as she put on an old pair of motoring gloves. Looking up, she saw briefly the flash of a light. Someone was on the moor. At this hour?

Or had it been her imagination? In the gloaming everything seemed different. Bullerton's residence looked tiny – more like a doll's house. She had lost her sense of direction – she could not find the section which would lead her up to the tunnel. She took a deep breath and the air was cold, which cleared her mind. The only solution was to climb up to the moor and explore, to search for the large round boulder she'd noticed near the entrance.

As she climbed, often on hands and knees, she was protected from the sharp rocky ground by her old jeans. One thing worried her: crawling up over shale, the small pieces started scattering down the slope, making too much noise.

She changed direction, moving gradually to her left, where the ground was more solid, more familiar. She thought she'd heard another noise above her, like a subdued moan. Could there be animals up here? If so, what were they? Reaching down she checked that her Browning was secure in its holster. The feel of the butt gave her fresh confidence.

She began hauling herself up more rapidly over the

ground, which was more stable than any so far. She was concentrating so determinedly on grasping tufts of grass, testing their stability before using them as handholds, that she got a shock.

Something spiky brushed her face. She stopped, looked up. It was the beginning of the black gorse. She stretched out a hand and touched something hard, smooth and round. She had located the large boulder near the entrance to the tunnel. She could have cheered.

She stood up, bent her aching knees several times. They still felt strong and limber. Crouching down, she crept slowly along the path, her left hand extended for fear of missing the tunnel entrance. Then she felt something odd. Taking off her glove, she felt with her bare hand a curved surface of smooth metal. She extracted her pencil torch from her backpack – her more powerful torch would show too much light in this wilderness. The brief illumination revealed a large circular lid covering the entrance to the tunnel. Putting on her glove again, she grasped a handle at the lid's top, twisted it slowly. It was well oiled and made not a sound as she removed it. The entrance was revealed. Using her more powerful torch she shone the beam inside it.

The entrance, easily large enough for her to crawl inside, was not inviting. The interior was clean but it gradually sloped downwards until, beyond the beam's reach, it was black as pitch.

'Come on, girl,' she said to herself, hitching the

pack onto her back and dropping to her knees to crawl inside. Her last hope was that Tweed had found the message shoved under his door.

When Tweed had ushered private detective Dermot Falkirk into his suite he immediately noticed a difference from the man he'd rescued from the cell in London. He was smartly dressed in a suit, his black hair had been cut, his moustache was shorter, neatly trimmed. His litheness was apparent in his movements but his normally poker face was smiling.

Using a technique rarely employed by other Yard interrogators, Tweed suggested Falkirk sat in the most comfortable armchair. At the Yard he would have been escorted to a bare room, seated in an uncomfortable hard-backed chair.

'How are you, Dermot?' Tweed asked, sitting in the other armchair.

'Exhausted.' Dermot grinned. 'I have a ton of information to give you. First, I'm breaking my code of secrecy. I have been employed by Miss Lisa Clancy, the only girl who escaped being murdered – her sisters, Nancy and Petra Mandeville, the two missing daughters of Lord Bullerton.'

'I have wondered recently if that's who they were,' Tweed said grimly. 'The daughter who employed you is Lizbeth Mandeville.'

'Yes,' Falkirk agreed, 'she changed her name when she escaped from Hobart House. She picked me out of the list of private detectives because she liked "Eyes Only". Don't ask me why. Mission, to locate the murderer of her sisters. Since I've broken the code and identified her I'll return the five thousand pounds she paid me.'

'What else did Lizbeth tell you? Incidentally, last night I called a friend at the Yard and she's under protection, but doesn't know it.'

'What else? She told me about this place, which was what sent me haring up to Hobartshire. On arrival I described Lisa to the landlord, pretending she'd flirted with me at a party down in London. He identified her as Lizbeth Mandeville.'

'Did Lizbeth tell you the whole story about leaving here?'

'Yes.' Falkirk smiled. 'After a little coaxing. They left to get away from her father. When they were much younger he'd bullied them and the late mother had been a strict disciplinarian. When they told Lord Bullerton he was appalled, gave each of them the sum of forty thousand pounds. They decided Lizbeth should just "disappear". Petra collected her clothes and arranged them neatly on the river bank. So she could have gone swimming and then drowned. They were pretty bitter according to Lizbeth. Well . . .' Falkirk shook his head. 'Not entirely.'

'Did she say what she did when she discovered the corpses?'

'Panicked. Rushed back into her house, locked and bolted the front door, switched off all the lights. That's when she saw, peering from behind a net curtain, the Rolls-Royce and amiable Mr Neville Guile.'

'That would be his first of two visits. Actually *saw* him?'

'Had his tinted glass window down, was peering out. She recognized him from a picture in a glossy magazine.'

'Know much about him?'

'Guile is the cruellest villain in Europe. Most murderous. Ruthless, callous and brutal. Adopts any method to succeed. Once he kidnapped the daughter of a Belgian banker who refused to sell his oil holdings. A message was sent to the banker that if he didn't sell within twenty-four hours the daughter would be returned. In pieces. The banker sold the oil holdings through an intermediary. The girl, unharmed but out of her wits with fear, was thrown from a car at the entrance to the banker's villa.'

'A very nasty piece of work,' Tweed commented.

'Yet he has a most remarkable personality, can charm the birds out of the trees, especially the female variety. Operates via third parties, so the police can never link him to his crimes.'

'So at present Lord Bullerton is his front man.'

'That's what I suspect,' Falkirk agreed. 'And Bullerton may have no idea of what is really going on.'

'*May*,' Tweed emphasized.

At that moment he saw the edge of the envelope Paula had pushed under his door. He opened it, read what she had written and thought for a moment. After her traumatic experience at the falls, then seeing the murdered Hartland Trent, she was probably exhausted, would sleep the night through.

Paula had dropped to her knees to explore the tunnel. When she risked shining her more powerful torch into the darkness the beam faded into blackness a few yards ahead. The tunnel must be endless. She had just entered when the metal buckle on her backpack scraped against the top of the tunnel. She worried about the noise, hauled the pack off her back and dragged it along by the handle. It was not long before the pressure of the unknown crept into her mind. She gritted her teeth, determined to discover the reason for the tunnel.

The tunnel continued its gradual descent. Soon she'd be deep under Black Gorse Moor. Not a pleasant thought. She was also worried that someone might find the lid entrance removed. Her back was completely exposed to attack. She paused frequently to listen.

The absolute silence was worse. It began to get on her nerves. She pressed on, crawling slowly. The hand which dragged her pack also held her powerful torch awkwardly, but she needed at least one hand free in case of emergency. Now the surface of the tunnel, still dropping, began to curve to her right so her torch could not illuminate what might lie ahead. She slowed her progress. Her outstretched left hand suddenly felt nothing beneath it. Dante's Inferno was nothing compared to this.

Her exploring left hand felt round the rim of nothing. She let go momentarily of her pack, aimed the torch, which had been wobbling all over the place. She had reached a vertical tunnel descending into the bowels of the earth. Beyond, her tunnel continued into darkness.

Easing herself forward inch by inch, she arrived at the rim of this new tunnel. She shone her torch down, almost dropped it in her shock. About eight feet down the beam was shining on the dead face of Archie MacBlade, body jammed into a space where the vertical tunnel narrowed. The eyes were closed.

'MacBlade!' she gasped in a whisper.

The eyes opened. One winked at her. That was when she heard voices, curiously distorted as they travelled down the extension of the vertical tunnel up to the moor. Instinctively she switched off her torch, hauled herself back a short distance from the rim. Despite the distortion, there was one voice she recognized immediately.

'You are quite clear what you have to do as soon as dawn comes?' the cut glass voice of Neville Guile demanded.

'Oh, I knows me business,' Ned Marsh, a wiry man with a hooked nose and a harelip, responded in his coarse voice.

'Then repeat your instructions and take that self-satisfied look off your ugly face.'

'At dawn I'll 'ave brought the truck of rubble and mud 'ere. I empty the flamin' lot down this tunnel. That bastard MacBlade will never be found.'

'Must be dead already,' Guile answered casually, 'after the blow from your cosh on the back of his head. And bring the truck along the top moor road. Time we moved off . . .'

Paula had held herself so still that after waiting to be sure they had gone she had to stretch. She shone her torch down inside the tunnel where MacBlade was trapped by the bulge in the wall. He called up to her in little more than a whisper.

'If I try to move I'll shift this soil bulge and drop twenty more feet. Bit of a problem, Paula.'

'Don't move an inch,' she whispered back. 'I've got an idea.'

The ingenious Harry had from time to time given her different equipment she might need. One item, stowed in her backpack, was a length of rope tightly knotted at three-foot intervals, and with a metal hook at one end covered with thick rubber. He'd told her it would 'come in handy' for entering the first floor of a target house. Lowering the rope, hooked end first, she told MacBlade what to do. As she talked, she wrapped the other end of the rope round her waist, praying she'd be strong enough to hold his weight. Twisting

Colin Forbes

her body round, she pressed both feet against the top of the tunnel where the metal surface was rougher. She peered over the edge, told him to come up when ready. MacBlade had followed her instructions to the letter. With the rubber-covered hook tucked inside his thick leather waist belt, he began hauling himself up, hands gripping a knot, then another. As soon as he moved, the soil bulge which had held him collapsed. Without the rope, he would have fallen at least twenty feet into the depths.

For Paula, the strain of his weight on her legs and shoulders was agonizing. She thanked God for her recent tough training exercise at the SIS mansion hidden on the Surrey border. She had stopped peering over the rim so was surprised at the speed with which MacBlade reached the top, fell across her, rolled off her and lay beside her, panting for breath.

They lay together like that for a while, exercising limbs and recovering. Then MacBlade squeezed her arm gently and asked, 'What next?'

'We get out of this fiendish tunnel. I know the way. I'll go first. Keep close behind me.'

'Gal, you've got guts,' he said.

'What's that plastic canister you've got in your pocket?'

'A sample. Let's start the crawl . . .'

As she eventually emerged from the tunnel she couldn't recall experiencing such a sense of relief. And now for the first time the moon had come out, illuminating the bowl far below. She screwed the lid back in position over the entrance, sat on it. MacBlade was stamping around in lively fashion.

'The Audi is parked in a hole in the hedge on this side of the road,' she told him. 'You make your way to it and I'll follow in a few minutes. Two people will be easier to spot in this moonlight.'

'Nothing doing,' he told her. 'You need protection – the least I can do after what you've done.'

'Do as you're damned well told!' she burst out. 'I need a few minutes on my own.'

'Then I'll wait over there.'

'For God's sake leave me alone,' she snapped, suddenly realizing she had raised her voice.

'Have it your own way,' he said with a warm smile and began walking away down from the moor into the bowl.

He had almost reached the bowl when once again he looked back. He wasn't able to see her: the hedge masked the round lid.

Paula stood up, stretched her legs and shoulders. A thick cloth hood descended over her head. Wiry hands swung her round, took hold of her wrists, clamped them in front of her with handcuffs. Then a familiar voice spoke with a cut-glass tone.

'She's all yours, Ned. Use her as a man likes to use a woman. Then kill her and bury the body. She knows too much.'

Paula found herself swung round, then frogmarched away from the moor. A wet cloth had been wrapped round her mouth so it was impossible to shout to MacBlade, who was probably too far away now. Where was she being taken by the lustful Ned Marsh?

13

Marsh's hands gripped her arms so tightly she knew it would be useless to struggle. He continued to propel her across a grassy surface. She had to be somewhere in the bowl which encircled Hobart House.

'You're goin' to enjoy this,' his coarse voice told her. 'At least the first part.'

'And the second part?' she said quietly.

'You won't know a thing. Guile is clever. He's seen you're Tweed's bit. When you disappear forever it will destroy your Mr Tweed. Guile knows he's the greatest danger.'

'Tweed will hunt you down, if he has to search the world for you . . .'

'Shut your face.'

Marsh's grip on her arms tightened painfully. They slowed down. She heard the squeak of a gate opening, felt her feet move off grass onto paving. She jerked her head up. The hood slipped back and she had a glimpse of the outside world.

She was looking up at a tiled cottage roof. A crooked chimney tilted down towards her. She knew where she was. Marsh rammed the hood back over her head. His tone was vicious.

'Don't get clever on me. We'll be longer on the bed.'

She knew where she was. She remembered seeing the tilted chimney across the bowl, the cottage almost hidden inside a copse of trees on the edge. Was this where Guile had remained out of sight for days? With Lord Bullerton's permission.

'Lift your clumsy feet,' Marsh ordered. 'We're going inside somewhere. Won't be long before you're flat on the bed. You lookin' forward to it? Be the last time you'll be with a man.'

She stumbled over a step and it was cooler. She was inside the cottage, being pushed along a wooden floor she assumed was the hall.

'Now you climb the stairs,' Marsh informed her. 'Slowly. Step by step, with me 'oldin' on to you. Nearly there for your last experience . . .'

Normally, whatever the danger, Paula remained calm and alert. For the first time in her life she was in a cold murderous fury. She remembered Neville Guile's words. *Use her as a man likes to use a woman.* She was incensed, in a killing mood.

She climbed the staircase carefully, feeling for the

next step before lifting a foot. Arriving at the top, Marsh guided her into a room, removed the hood, flung her onto the double bed. She was careful to fall on her back, sprawling her legs along the sheet. Marsh had made one fatal mistake.

He stood at the end of the bed, stripped off his jacket, then his shirt. He was grinning evilly. She lay with her cuffed hands and the long metal chain between them over the lower part of her body.

'You can stretch your arms,' he said with a leer. 'They're in the way.'

She raised both arms behind her head as he sprawled on top of her. Her hands whipped down, over his head, round his neck, were winding the chain, long enough, thank God, to encircle his throat. She crossed her hands within seconds, pulled them outwards. The chain bit deep into his windpipe. She increased the pressure. The chain dug deeper.

He was choking. His hands, which might otherwise have been used to beat at her body, flew up to his throat, fingers desperately trying to insert themselves under the chain but the metal links were buried too tightly. Coldly, she watched him fighting for breath which couldn't enter the windpipe. She felt his feet and legs hammering on the bed. He opened his mouth but no words emerged. She pulled the chain a fraction tighter and his face was changing colour. Then the hammering of feet and legs ceased. His hands, which had been clawing at the chain, fell to his sides. He was very still. She held on. To be sure. His body had slumped, lifeless, on hers.

She eased herself from beneath him after lifting the chain. She rubbed her hands to bring back circulation, rolled his body to the edge of the bed, dipped her hand into the pocket of his shirt on the floor where she had seen him tuck the handcuff key.

Her hands trembled but she managed to unlock the cuffs, which she dropped on the floor, kicking them under the bed. As a final precaution she checked his carotid artery. No pulse. Pushing the body off the bed, she shoved it underneath.

She found a small bathroom, turned the cold-water tap, soaked her face and hands. She wiped her fingerprints off the tap, collected from the stairs the motoring gloves she had surreptitiously dropped, left the cottage and started walking across the bowl on stiffish legs to where she had parked the Audi. Vaguely, seeing lights in Hobart House, she wondered whether Tweed was still dining with Lord Bullerton.

'My God, where have you been?'

It was MacBlade's voice, but she nearly jumped out of her skin. He told her Harry had turned up on foot out of nowhere and was guarding the vehicle. Arriving at the parked Audi she told both of them in short sentences what had happened. Harry reacted immediately, turning to MacBlade.

'Give me a hand to remove the body from the cottage?'

'Sure thing. You OK to drive back to the hotel, Paula?'

'What I could do with. A nice quiet drive back to the hotel.'

Arriving back at the hotel, she parked the Audi, was surprised to realize she was ravenously hungry. She took off her smeared tunic and jeans, washed, brushed her hair and went downstairs.

She dined alone. The food was excellent and she devoured a three-course meal. Arriving back at her suite she forced herself to take a quick shower. Afterwards she couldn't be bothered to get into her night attire. Her last thought before she fell into a deep sleep was how Tweed had fared during his dinner with Lord Bullerton.

14

Earlier in the evening, Tweed was driven to Hobart House by Harry in his Fiat. Harry left his chief at the foot of the steps, drove the car round the back

Tweed had adopted a tactic he'd used before, catching people on the wrong foot by arriving early. The door was opened for him by an elegantly dressed Mrs Shipton. Her dark hair was piled on top of her head. He thought he detected fairish strands. Her shapely body was encased firmly in a green dress with a wide gold belt emphasizing her narrow waist.

'You are early,' she greeted him with an inviting smile. 'We could have time for a drink. Lord Bullerton is ensconced in his study. Shall we use the library?'

Intrigued by the warmth of her approach, Tweed followed her into the library. The lights were dim so he chose a couch as the nearest place to sit. She must have used the dimmer because the lights came on more strongly.

'Wine?' she enquired. 'Red or white. Or maybe Scotch?'

'White wine, please.'

Standing by the wine cabinet her face was in profile. Tweed wondered where he had seen that Roman nose before. With the drinks on a silver tray she returned, placed the tray on a coffee table, sat on the couch close to him. She crossed her legs and raised her glass.

'To success.'

'I'll drink to that,' Tweed agreed. He sipped his wine and placed his glass on the table. 'I'm curious as to what part of the world you come from.'

'That's something I never discuss. I was glad to get away.'

'You have a good position here?'

'I see to it that it is. Lord Bullerton may not be the easiest man to work for but I make sure that the relationship works. After his wife, Myra, fell from the falls he had no one to look after this place. A friend of mine in Gunners Gorge, who has gone abroad, tipped me off. So I came to see him.'

'Was it an easy encounter?'

'Not for him.' She chuckled. 'Said he'd pay me the earth when I expressed doubt. I asked him how much the earth cost.'

'And his reaction?'

'He bellowed with laughter, then offered me the generous sum which I wanted.'

Tweed stood up, walked over to a wall where a gilt-framed picture was turned to the wall. He reversed it. The painting was of a woman with her back turned while her face peered over her shoulder where two large substantial wings were attached.

'Would this be his late wife, Myra?' he enquired.

'Yes.'

'I noticed last time I was here the painting was turned to face the wall. Why?'

'It gets dusty on the glass,' she said quickly.

He smeared a finger over the whole of the glass, showed it to her as she shuffled her feet. He smiled.

'Not a trace of dust,' he commented. He studied the profile, turned to face her. 'Seems a bit odd.'

'Well,' she said, approaching, her voice harder, 'do you think it would be a good thing for him to brood over memories of the past?'

'I suppose not. He doesn't mind it facing the wall?'

'He leaves me to run the house in my own way. That was one of the conditions I imposed when accepting the post. Your drink is waiting for you.'

Tweed walked back to the coffee table, picked up his drink and avoided the couch. Instead he sat in an armchair in front of an antique refectory table. Mrs Shipton came back, stood up. He gathered she was not pleased.

The door opened and Lance strolled in, a striking figure in a dinner jacket. Tweed glanced over his shoulder. The painting of Myra had been turned round again, her face to the wall.

'Mrs Shipton,' Lance said in his most lofty tone, 'Cook is in trouble with the soufflé. She's worried it's going to collapse.'

'Oh, hell, everything in this place goes to pieces if I'm not on hand . . .'

Without a word to Tweed, Mrs Shipton hurried from the library. Lance walked forward, sat in a hard-backed chair opposite Tweed. He touched the lapel of his dinner jacket.

'If you don't object I'd like to join the dinner. I'm hoping my father won't mind.'

'Up to you. I'm only a guest, and Miss Grey was unable to come,' Tweed replied.

As he said this he reached down for the slim executive case he always carried with him. For the first time he extracted the photographs Hector Humble had produced after building up the faces of the two women murdered in London. Face down he pushed them over the table.

'Can you tell me who these two people are?'

Lance turned them over, stared at the photos. His face turned ashen. For a moment he slumped in his chair, then made an effort and straightened up again. He gazed at Tweed, his almond eyes glazed. He tapped one photo, then the other.

'This is Nancy, this is Petra, two of my missing sisters. When were these pictures taken?'

'After they had been brutally murdered in London, both faces horribly gouged with some unknown instrument.'

'I don't understand,' Lance said aggressively. 'There's no sign of mutilation on these photos.'

'Taken,' Tweed said mildly, 'after a brilliant man had built them up again.'

'Sounds macabre to—'

He never completed his sentence. The door was flung open and Lord Bullerton, dressed in a business suit, burst into the room. He stared at Lance and his voice boomed.

'You can take off the penguin suit, Lance. This dinner will be between me and Mr Tweed. So may I suggest you shove off.'

'You see how it is,' Lance muttered, stood up and left. At the door he had to wait as Mrs Shipton reappeared. Staring at Lance's dinner jacket, she frowned. He heard what she said as he pushed rudely past her.

'On Lord Bullerton's instructions I have prepared dinner for two persons.'

'Is it ready?' demanded Bullerton.

'Yes. That is, it will be in ten minutes' time.'

While all this was going on Tweed retrieved the two photos. He slipped them carefully inside, closed the zip. Only then, case under his arm, did he stand up to greet his host.

'Excuse me, Tweed,' Bullerton said, 'my obsession is chess. I am trying to crack this game. Would you like another drink?'

'I'll wait for dinner, thank you.'

He watched as Bullerton hurried over to a table where a chess game was half-played. Seating himself, he picked up the Queen, turning to Tweed as he fondled the piece. He shook his head.

'She's the one I'm after. I play against myself. Unless you care to oppose me. Dinner will take longer than Mrs Shipton implied. She won't bring in the food until all the guests have taken their places. Shipton rules.'

'I prefer to start a fresh game, if you don't mind,' said Tweed, standing up. He extracted the two photos and again placed them upside down on the edge of the chess table.

'I thought, Lord Bullerton, these might be familiar to you.'

The effect on his host was even more electrifying than it had been on Lance. Bullerton casually turned them over, bent his large head forward, then jumped up, staggering as though he might fall down. Tweed grabbed him by one arm, had his grip brusquely removed. Bullerton toppled backwards into the armchair behind him and slumped. His voice was hoarse when he spoke.

'Large Scotch, for God's sake!'

Tweed darted over to the drinks cupboard, grabbed a glass and a bottle of the most expensive Scotch. He filled the large glass, took it to Bullerton, watched carefully as his host took the glass, swallowed half the contents at one gulp. He waited as Bullerton sat up stiffly, drank the rest.

'One is Petra,' he mumbled, 'the other is Nancy. Where are they now?'

146

'In London.' Tweed paused. 'The news is very bad, I should warn you . . .'

'You bastard!' Bullerton roared. 'How long have you had those?'

'Only a day,' Tweed admitted, 'I was waiting for the right opportunity to tell you – when we were alone. The news is bad,' he repeated.

'Well, spit it out, man,' Bullerton demanded, some of his normal fire returning.

'They are both dead,' Tweed said quietly, 'murdered outside the homes they rented in central London. Worse still, their faces had been badly mutilated by the killer.'

'Mutilated?' Bullerton pointed to the photos Tweed was collecting to put back inside his case. 'No sign of mutilation there.'

'The photos have been retouched,' said Tweed, who saw no point in explaining the genius of Hector Humble.

'Sounds like a serial killer.'

As he spoke Bullerton bent down to pick up the chess Queen he had knocked off the board when he jumped up. He stroked the piece as he muttered half to himself.

'She knows I'm after seducing her. Just like I do when I visit certain high-class ladies in Mayfair. They charge the earth. Still much cheaper than the expense of getting married. This Queen seems to get heavier. Ready for my assault. And you're a fake, Tweed. You come up here on a murder investigation but you take

147

your time telling me the victims are my missing daughters.'

'I have my methods,' Tweed said calmly. 'And I do not believe the killer is a serial murderer . . .'

'Obviously you haven't heard that Hartland Trent, living, or lived, off the High Street has been found stabbed to death. Whole district is abuzz with the crime, but the chief investigator hasn't heard about it,' Bullerton sneered. 'An eccentric. The place swarms with them.'

Tweed was used to the minds of relatives of murder victims wandering all over the place in their shock.

'Another eccentric, the chief one, is Mrs Grout in the Village. A few years ago a crazy man bought a farm well north of the River Lyne, converted it into a zoo! Had a huge gorilla, a king cobra, a tiger and Lord knows what else. Oh, a crocodile too. I got the correct lot up from London and they closed him down. What helped was the local horsey aristocrats living in that area protested violently, saying one of the creatures in the zoo could escape and kill someone. The owner was venomous, swore vengeance, but sent his stock to Africa and India. Mrs Grout made a meal of it.'

'How did she do that?'

'She still tells some crazy story that she saw the zoo owner one moonlit night drive a truck to the edge of the river north of the bridge, open the doors, slide out a chute with the baby crocodile inside and dump it in the river. She's mad.'

'How long ago did this happen?'

'About three years, except it's just one of her stories.'

'So by now it would be fully grown,' Tweed remarked.

'Suppose so, wherever it is in India . . .'

The door opened and Mrs Shipton stood there, glaring. Her arms were folded. She barked.

'If you like cold food you can stay here chattering. It will be served in the dining room within five minutes.'

Bullerton hauled his bulk out of the armchair as the door was slammed shut. They walked to the dining room, which was tastefully illuminated by a magnificent chandelier that might have come from Versailles. They ate in silence, which suited Tweed, so he could enjoy the excellent dinner. He waited until they were sipping a first-class claret before he put the question.

'I had wondered whether Neville Guile might be another guest.'

'Told me he was going to race back to London. That the countryside bored him. Typical view of the average Londoner.'

'You like him? He seems to have achieved a lot.'

'Like so many London businessmen he's a crook. But in business you have to deal with all types '

'I do know a number of businessmen who are trustworthy,' Tweed corrected him.

'Then don't count Neville among them.'

'Do you mind if I ask the nature of your dealings with him?'

'Sorry, but our negotiations are confidential. I do assure you, Mr Tweed, that it can have nothing to do with these awful murders.' He paused, embarrassed. 'One thing I will tell you. Neville had consumed a lot of brandy at eleven in the morning. I think he let his tongue slip. Told me he was going back to Finden Square to clear up the mess he knew he'd find. Then he was flying off to what he calls his sanctuary, the island of Noak.' He spelt out the name. 'Sounds like Noah's Ark. It's somewhere not a million miles from the Channel Islands. Not under the jurisdiction of either Britain or France. When he told me he laughed – that weird giggle which passes for a laugh.'

'I think it's time I left. Thank you for the most glorious dinner. As good as the Ritz in London,' Tweed said, pushing back his chair.

'I suppose,' Bullerton remarked as they strolled towards the door, 'as chief investigator you'll be involved in the Trent murder here. With my two eldest daughters as victims the serial killer has moved up to Hobartshire. Not a pleasant thought.'

'My instinct, experience if you like, tells me all I need is to spot the motive. When I do I'll know who the killer is.'

15

The next morning a carefully dressed but nervous Paula tapped the agreed tattoo on Tweed's door. Wearing a sports jacket and grey slacks, he ushered her inside with a smile and a wave of his hand. He immediately noticed her unusually worried expression.

'Come in. Make yourself at home,' he greeted her cheerfully.

She sat down in a hard-backed chair, her feet together. She sat very erect, spoke softly.

'I have something to tell you I don't think you'll like.'

'A cup of steaming black coffee might help start the day.'

He poured her a cup and tactfully placed it on a small table next to her chair. He guessed she might have trouble not spilling it as she lifted the cup.

'I think we ought to have a full breakfast up here. I'll order it,' he said firmly, reaching for the phone.

'Won't the landlord think it funny I'm in your suite so early?' she ventured.

'Mr Bowling has been running this hotel for a long time, I'm sure. He'll be quite used to serving breakfasts to men who have spent the night with a lady friend. Par for the course.'

Over the phone he ordered a huge breakfast for two, to be served in twenty minutes. Tea, more coffee, toast – white and brown (which he knew Paula preferred), scrambled eggs for two, crispy bacon, toasted muffins . . .

'We'll both be fighting fit after that,' he said, refilling her cup. 'Now, I'll just listen.'

She told him of the events of the previous night, starting with her driving the Audi from the hotel and parking it inside the hedge overlooking Hobart House. She kept it brief and found herself talking more quickly as Tweed kept nodding his head to show her he was taking it all in. His expression was pleasant, that of the interested listener – until she came to the point where she quoted what Neville Guile had said to his henchman. *Use her as a man likes to use a woman*.

His lips tightened. He turned his head away so Paula would not see the cold fury in his eyes. From that moment on he couldn't wait until he met Neville Guile in a quiet place and slowly strangled him.

He lit a rare cigarette and when he turned to face

Paula again his expression of listening to every word she said had returned. She concluded with her walking away from the cottage with the crooked chimney back across the bowl to the parked car.

'I'm sorry,' she said. 'I should never have taken the risk . . .'

'Wrong!' he exploded. 'You were right. Haven't I always told every member of the team they must use their initiative? Which is exactly what you did. It may have been pretty grim for you, but you proved you can – and do – think for yourself.'

'Thank you,' she said quietly.

'The next problem is to get rid of the body of the fiend who attacked you.'

'It's already been done. On my way along the corridor to get here I met Harry. He said the thug's name was Ned Marsh – he found his passport on his body in the cottage. With the help of Archie MacBlade he carried the body back up to Black Gorse Moor, found the tunnel I'd been in and the vertical drop. They dumped the body down the tunnel – it went all the way down. MacBlade said Guile is always checking. When he phones Marsh on his mobile during the night and gets no reply he'll send another thug at once to drive the truck. Half a ton of rubble will be emptied down the tunnel. The thug who tried to rape and kill me will never be found.'

'Solves one problem,' Tweed commented.

'I'm perplexed,' said Paula. 'Nothing links up. Mystery One – Harry tracks Falkirk up here. We follow. Mystery Two – we find Hartland Trent murdered, his place ransacked. Mystery Three – how does Lord Bullerton fit in? Mystery Four – why is Neville Guile visiting this part of the world? Then, what is happening on Black Gorse Moor with that network of tunnels?'

'You left out one more,' Tweed remarked. 'Who really hired Falkirk, private detective?'

'And,' she added, 'I haven't seen Chief Inspector Roadblock for some time.'

Tweed chuckled. 'That's because I phoned Buchanan and asked him to recall the gentleman to London. His new task? To call at every residence in the Lynton Avenue area to ask if they saw anything. He gets no reply since they're on holiday. He has to persist until he meets them.'

'Which will take him forever. All those houses.'

'That's my idea. Can't have him up here messing up the whole case. But our main task remains the same – to identify the murderer.'

'Any suspects yet?' she coaxed.

'I think a large part of the motive is Black Gorse Moor.'

The pleasant maid had cleared the breakfast clutter, but Paula was still puzzled by Tweed's reply. Another factor entered her mind. She looked across to where Tweed was perched on the edge of his bed, studying his notebook.

'Noak Island. Could that be important? Somewhere remote out in the Atlantic?'

'All great minds think alike.' He smiled. 'I was just wondering about that myself.'

'And there's a strange item in the paper. Something about Asiatic pirates who grabbed a big oil tanker, fully laden, about seven months ago.'

'I spotted that too.'

Tweed stopped talking as someone rapped on the door.

He had his Walther behind his back as he unlocked the door. Outside Archie MacBlade stood with Falkirk. MacBlade smiled as he politely put the question.

'Any chance of our having a confidential chat now?'

'Perfect timing. I have Paula with me. Come in. Seat yourselves while I listen.'

MacBlade chose a large couch after hugging Paula, asking how she was, whether she had slept well.

'Very OK,' she said with a warm smile. 'Slept solidly the whole night through.'

Falkirk had joined MacBlade on the couch. MacBlade waved a hand at his companion.

'Think it was time I came clean. I was the one who hired our mutual ally, Falkirk.'

16

'I'm stunned,' said Paula.

'Why?' asked Tweed.

'I'd never have guessed that in a hundred years,' she exclaimed.

'*Why?*' demanded Tweed.

'Because,' MacBlade explained, 'I needed someone first-rate to check on Neville Guile, to find out everything he could about the villain. I could hardly come to you, Tweed – not with you running your own show, as you always do. We've been discussing Guile's secret island, Noak. The mysterious Noak out on the Gulf Stream.'

'Could be idyllic,' Paula mused. 'Palm trees and coconuts.'

'Or something grimmer,' said Falkirk, with a warm smile.

It was the first time she'd seen Falkirk relax. She found she was beginning to like this tough lean-faced man.

'I need every bit of information you've dug up,' Tweed said very seriously.

There was another tapping on his door. Again he concealed his Walther behind his back before unlocking the door. Marler was standing outside with a long cardboard roll tucked under his arm. Tweed lowered his voice.

'I have Archie MacBlade and Falkirk with me. Paula too. We are beginning to discuss Neville Guile's secret island, Noak.'

'Which is why I've come to see you. I now know a lot about how to get to the place. There are traps.'

'You'd better come in and join the party, then.'

Introductions were swiftly over. Marler laid the cardboard roll on the cleared table they were now gathered round.

He looked at Tweed for a signal.

'Do I reveal everything I've discovered?'

'Everything,' Tweed assured him.

'This map,' Marler began, 'I obtained from a mariner friend high up in his service. They know of the island's existence but do not know it belongs to Neville Guile. Here goes . . .'

From the cardboard roll he extracted a large map, spreading it to flatten it. Paula immediately recognized it as showing the western coast of Brittany, the Channel Islands, a vast stretch of the Atlantic with another island well to the west of the Channel Islands group. The island was circled in red.

Near the bottom of the large sheet was another map, a detailed outline of Noak. A drawing on this map showed steep cliffs and a section of dotted lines shaped like a triangle with the narrowed apex ending at a gulch. Marler pointed to the dotted lines projecting into the Atlantic.

'That's the trap,' he explained. 'Guile has sophisticated radar which picks up any vessel approaching Noak.'

'Is there a gap covering a landing point invisible to this radar system, maybe caused by the high overhanging cliffs?'

'Clever girl,' Marler said with an admiring smile. 'That is where we land without Guile knowing we've arrived. Tricky, but I could manage it.' He looked round the table. 'Presumably the vessel available will be crewed by me and Falkirk?'

'No,' snapped Tweed. 'Has it ample capacity for more people?'

'Yes. It's very roomy. Has a small stateroom.'

'Then it will also be crewed, as you put it, by me, Paula and Harry. We need power in case we come up against guards.'

'True.' Marler stood up, the map rolled and back in its case. 'I've got things to arrange, consult someone about weapons.' Both Tweed and Paula knew he meant Harry, but was being typically cautious since MacBlade and Falkirk were present. He turned at the door.

'Timetable? I can be ready within two days, even by tomorrow.'

'In case of emergency think of tomorrow,' Tweed decided.

MacBlade and Falkirk left soon after him. Paula waited until they were alone before she voiced her doubts.

'Aren't we leaving Gunners Gorge before we've checked it out thoroughly?'

'Yes, we are,' Tweed agreed. 'But Neville Guile is one of a number of strong suspects. I need to find out what he's up to on this mysterious island of Noak. He's rushed off, and my instinct is that he's on his way there.'

'What's next today, then?'

'A visit by both of us to Hobart House. I want to interrogate Bullerton's two daughters, Sable and Margot. Girls can be very observant.' He smiled. 'They have been known to listen unseen at closed doors . . .'

'I don't like that knife Margot carried concealed in a sheath.'

'Also,' Tweed continued, 'I'd like to grill Mrs Shipton. Something's not right about her. I asked the landlord where she came from. He said out of the blue, no idea where. A year or two after Myra had her so-called accident and went over the falls.'

Inside the garage they found a livid Lord Bullerton

pacing back and forth. He addressed Tweed abruptly.

'Would you believe it? My fool of a chauffeur has taken my car to the mechanic way north of the bridge beyond the Gorge. Didn't consult me – just left a note. I'll have his guts for garters!'

'Where were you going?' Tweed enquired.

'Just back to Hobart House. But it's one hell of a walk.'

'We're going there in my car,' Tweed told him. 'Give you a lift.'

'There are some gentlemen left in this mess of a world,' he growled. 'I accept your offer gratefully.'

Paula opened the front passenger door of the Audi, gestured with a smile. He quietened down, gave her a grateful warm smile, climbed aboard as she closed the door and parked herself in the back seat as Tweed took over behind the wheel.

As they were approaching the country road turn-off to Hobart House they saw Mrs Grout watering plant pots placed on either side of her red front door. Bullerton pointed at her and snorted contemptuously.

'Barmy old bag. *Crocodiles!*'

17

Margot opened the front door, Bullerton pushed past her, calling over his shoulder that he had a pile of work waiting in his study. Margot had to jump aside to avoid being knocked over.

'Good morning, Margot,' Tweed greeted her with a warm smile. 'I need to talk to just you and Sable.'

'Do we have to drag in Sable?'

'I do need to talk to the two of you together. No one else present.'

'OK. Sable's in the library. Not in the best of moods, so life is normal,' she concluded with a mischievous grin. As they reached the library door she paused. 'That was catty of me. I erase the remark . . .'

She was smartly turned out, wearing white roll-neck jumper, a checked pleated skirt, sensible flat-heeled shoes.

'Company, Sable,' she announced as they entered.

Scowling, Sable sat at a desk with papers spread untidily over its surface, her blonde head bent over them.

'Tell them to go to hell,' she rasped. 'I'm busy with university homework.' Then she looked up, saw who the visitors were. Her attitude was transformed. The scowl was replaced by a flashing welcoming smile. Jumping up, she ran to Tweed, threw both arms round him, hugged a little too passionately, watching Margot over his shoulder.

Releasing him she held out her hand to Paula, squeezed it warmly. Leading them both to a couch, she ignored Margot. She was taking control.

'Drinks?' she offered as they sat down. 'I'm on vodka – helps me plough through dull work. Vodka for both of you? Or coffee or tea?' She glared at Margot. 'What are you hanging around for? They've come to see me.'

'Actually,' Tweed said firmly, 'I need to talk to both of you together. And I'd like a small glass of Chardonnay, if that's possible.'

'For me too,' Paula said quickly.

'Coming up . . .'

Sable was more daringly dressed than her sister. As she bent to fetch a bottle, bending to a lower shelf, her short skirt rode up, exposing most of her excellent legs. Her blouse dipped, showing the tops of two well-shaped bosoms. She came back with two glasses on a silver tray.

'I think I'll have Chardonnay too,' Margot chipped in.

'Well, you know where the bottle is,' snapped Sable but Margot was already helping herself.

When she came back she sat next to Paula. She adjusted her skirt to cover her elegant knees. Sable was now seated in an imposing carver chair on the other side of the desk, elevated above them.

'Cheers!' said Margot, raising her glass. 'Now, how can we help you?'

'I have detected in this house an atmosphere of unease,' Tweed began. 'Have you any idea what causes it? One person? If so, who?'

'This is a house of hatred,' Sable burst out. 'We all have to fight our corner to survive,' she said viciously. 'Father is a problem. Sometimes moody – once said he wished we'd never been born . . .'

'That's a wild exaggeration,' Margot protested.

'At other times he's so generous with presents.' She touched the expensive diamond brooch attached to her blouse, gazed maliciously at Margot.

'I'd say,' Margot insisted, 'we're just an average family who have disagreements now and again.'

'Bollocks!' Sable burst out again.

'Our guests are accustomed to using decent language,' Margot said quietly.

'All right!' Sable shouted, then quietened down. 'I apologize for using the word.' She glared at Margot. 'It would be my older sister to pick me up on that.'

'I'm one year older than Sable,' Margot said, again quietly.

'What do you both think of your brother, Lance?' Tweed asked.

'He's a pain—' Sable began.

'He keeps to himself,' Margot explained. 'Understandable being so out-numbered by sisters.'

'Does he go to London frequently?' Tweed said, speaking rapidly, determined to get quick answers before either sister could think.

'Frequently,' replied Margot.

'When he's not fooling around with the local talent,' sneered her sister.

'I gather he's determined under no circumstances to be the next Lord Bullerton . . .'

'Inside this house,' Sable said. 'But he keeps quiet in the Village, in Gunners Gorge and round the country-side.'

'Why would he do that?' rapped out Tweed.

'Because,' Sable said with an unpleasant grin, 'it impresses the aristo girls he lures to his flat. The clots think it's great to spend a night or two with the future Lord Bullerton.'

'*Aristo* girls?' queried Tweed.

'Members of the aristocracy,' Sable explained. 'The horsey set. Quite a few are my friends so I hear what's going on. Margot is never asked to their parties,' she concluded triumphantly.

'Don't know them,' Margot remarked coolly. 'Don't want to. I don't like horses. Don't ride. Bit of a bore.'

'Fact is,' Sable elaborated as she hitched her jumper higher, 'no one would dream of inviting her. Not their circle.'

'Where does Mrs Shipton come from?' Tweed asked suddenly.

He's using his tactic, Paula thought, of changing the subject without warning to throw people off balance.

'Mrs Shipton?' Sable echoed vaguely.

'Yes, Mrs Shipton,' Tweed repeated emphatically. 'My question was clear enough.' He turned to Margot, who nodded before she replied.

'We really have no idea. She just turned up when Father was desperate for someone to run the house.'

'So,' Sable broke in, annoyed that the attention had swung away from her, 'he offered her the crown jewels by way of a salary and she accepted. As to where she comes from I have no damned idea. Oh, excuse me.'

'You have both been most helpful,' Tweed said, rising. 'I am grateful for the time you've given us. Tomorrow Paula and I are travelling to London for a couple of days before we come back. I have to check the situation at HQ.'

They had reached the closed door when Sable darted ahead of them so beat Margot to opening it. Tweed pressed one hand against it and fired his last shot. 'Lord Bullerton, does he often travel to London?'

'Very often,' Sable said before Margot could reply, 'says he's going on business for a few days.' She smirked. 'I've seen the business, so-called. I was in Mayfair once, saw him chatting up an attractive woman in a tight dress. Then they disappeared together into a very expensive block of flats where the "lady" probably has a suite. I suppose he has to have his fling regularly. Bet it's a different woman each time. He's too smart to risk being tied to one woman even for what he's needing, being a man.'

Glancing back as they left the room, Paula saw Margot with her eyes raised to heaven at Sable's crude way of expressing herself. She gave Paula a lovely smile and a little wave of her hand.

'Was it worth it?' Paula asked as they drove away.

'I found it very significant what Margot said, even more so what Sable said.'

'And you're not going to tell me yet?'

'Not until I'm sure I'm right. Incidentally, how long would it take you to get packed for immediate departure?'

'One minute. I'm always packed for any emergency.'

'Good. Because as soon as we get back to the Nag's Head we're driving south to Marler's boat and sailing to Noak. That talk about leaving tomorrow was camouflage. I'm sure Sable won't be able to help spilling the beans to someone. Marler has been alerted. He's warned Harry. I don't want MacBlade or Falkirk to know . . .'

As they arrived back at the garage, Marler appeared from nowhere with Harry. He told Tweed they were ready to leave now. Looking at Paula he smiled.

'Hope you don't mind riding as my passenger in my Maserati – on the motorway for a lot of the trip.'

'I'd love that,' she fibbed as her stomach flipped.

'Tweed drives the Audi with the armour plate and armoured glass, taking Harry as passenger.'

He broke off as Lance walked in from the hotel. He wore a long white pullover and plaid trousers. He greeted them with a warm smile.

'Off somewhere, are we?'

'To London. Tomorrow,' Tweed said quickly. 'We're checking the state of our transport.'

'You'll be coming back, I hope?'

'At the latest two days after tomorrow,' Tweed assured him.

'I mustn't linger. Busy day ahead of me.'

As he spoke he jumped on a brand-new Harley-Davidson motorbike and left the garage at speed, driving up the High Street. Paula watched him as he pulled in at a house halfway up the street, ran to the door, which was opening. A tall well-built blonde appeared holding a shopping carrier. She kissed him, he patted her on the rump, she walked away as he closed the door.

'Another *aristo* victim,' Paula commented. 'Bet he's packing her bag, ready to dump it on the doorstep . . .'

'I've got the special weapons you suggested,' Harry reported to Tweed.

Colin Forbes

'Time to move,' said Tweed. '*Now!*' He looked at Marler. 'I'd like to know where we're going.'

'Seaward Cove, border of Somerset and Devon. We'll be there before night. Cove is remote, size of an oyster shell . . .'

18

With Marler at the wheel and Paula beside him, Hobartshire passed in a flash as they headed south. Turning onto the motorway, Marler pressed his foot down. They *flew*.

As far as Paula could tell, Marler kept just within all speed limits – she knew he had an instinct for speed traps. The drive was an experience she would never forget. Scenery passed in a blur – rolling green hills, a dense wood, a vast rocky quarry where strange machines prowled. Marler, wearing tinted goggles, had long ago passed her a pair to counter the searchlight glare of the sun burning out of an endless blue sky.

Some time before, Marler had turned south-west. Paula's thick glossy black hair was streaming out behind her. She found a pink ribbon, tied her hair into a ponytail. Later Marler pointed to a plastic box.

'Food,' he said abruptly.

She extracted thick salmon sandwiches, fed Marler as he continued driving, then herself. There was Evian water to quench their thirst. By now Paula was relaxed. I could get used to driving like this, she thought.

Occasionally she glanced in the rear-view mirror, at first surprised to find the heavy armoured Audi was only a hundred yards behind them, then remembering Harry had souped up its engine.

'Can you find out,' she asked Marler, 'when we are about half an hour from our destination?'

'You ask Ben,' he said, handing her his mobile after pressing umpteen buttons.

'Ben here. Who the hell is this?' a rough voice answered.

She identified them, giving the name of a winding village Marler had been compelled to crawl through. The rough voice wasted no time.

'Thirty minutes from now, the way Marler drives.'

Paula contacted Tweed on her mobile, which he still possessed. Her reminder was short. 'Paula here. The bottle, Tweed. *Now!*'

In the Audi, Tweed reached for the twist of paper inside which he had folded a Dramamine tablet. Tactfully, Harry handed him a bottle of Evian water without a word. Tweed swallowed the tablet.

The one aversion Tweed had was the sea. He disliked even looking at it from firm land. 'It never stops wobbling about,' he had once explained to Paula. She knew this and always persuaded her chief to take precautions.

'How much further, I wonder?' speculated Harry. 'The sun is dropping into lower orbit.'

'Another thirty minutes and we're there,' Tweed replied. 'I gather we arrive just before dusk and go aboard the *Tiger* as soon as we get there.'

'The *Tiger*?'

'Name of the ship we travel on.'

'Don't like the sound of it.'

'Join the club,' Tweed commented.

'Are we travelling on a big ship?' Paula asked Marler.

'Surprisingly big. Even has a luxury stateroom. Compact but cosy.'

'How did Ben afford such a vessel?'

'Ben fished for prawns,' Marler chuckled. 'Off the cove there's a whole fleet of them. Biggest you've ever seen. He makes a fortune selling them to top London restaurants. Look at one of their menus. Prawns head the list for price.'

Marler stopped talking as the landscape changed dramatically. Great granite bluffs reared up out of scrubby grass on both sides. Vaguely it reminded Paula of pictures she had seen of Utah, but minus the columnar chimneys of stone. Here and there a stubborn pine with a massive trunk lent a touch of green.

Marler slowed as they climbed a ridge on the narrowing tarmacadam road. Once they crossed the ridge, the road dropped steeply. Paula almost gasped at the view of the vast sea which stretched forever towards a distant horizon. It was dusk and the sun, which had slid below the horizon, seemed to illuminate the Channel from below with a weird aquamarine glow.

'There it is. Seaward Cove,' Marler told her.

'That's a cove?' she asked in disbelief.

She was looking down on a gash, long and narrow, piercing the massive cliffs. Projecting from the shore was a large stone jetty, curved like a sickle, presumably to take the force of giant waves in a storm. Moored to its inner wall was a large slim ship with a small funnel.

'Ben can't get that ship out of that channel,' she protested.

'He will. Only way out.'

She was relieved from Tweed's point of view that the ocean was more like a flat blue plate: not a ripple in sight. They reached the landing point in no time. Tweed's Audi parked behind them.

A short heavily built man in his fifties with a very wide chest came out of a large shed. He shook hands only with Paula, pointed to the shed.

'That's home and where I prepare the prawns for despatch to London.' He looked at Marler. 'Four hours I calculate to get to this invisible Noak Island, four to get back, so how long you gonna be foolin' around there?'

'About one hour, maybe longer. Depends on the element of danger,' Tweed told the old ruffian.

'*Danger!*' Ben glared at Marler. 'You never said a

thing about that. Cost you another ten thousand quid on top of the fee.'

'Come off it,' Marler told Ben with a grin. 'You know that anything I'm involved in can turn ugly.'

'All right.' Ben cupped his hands round his mouth. 'All of you aboard. We have to be back here before dawn. Jump to it!'

Paula ran forward, skipped up the gangplank, ignoring Ben's shout. 'Hold on to the flamin' rails!'

He pulled his peaked cap lower over his broad forehead. This time he kept his voice down as he spoke to Tweed as he was about to go aboard.

'That girl is agile! – and very tough, I suspect.'

'She's in her thirties,' Tweed retorted and ran up the gangway.

He followed her along a companionway, through an open door, down some steps into a luxurious stateroom. She sprawled on a comfortable couch at the other end. They heard voices from the dock.

'What's in that big bag, mate?'

'My lunch,' Harry's voice shouted back. 'Put a sock in it and get this old tub moving . . .'

Ben appeared at the entrance to the stateroom. He pointed forward.

'Galley's at that end. Fridge is jam-packed. You could cook us some plaice and chips. OK?'

'If I feel like it,' Paula snapped back.

Minutes later they felt movement. *Tiger* was about to navigate the impossible channel. As the ship swung round to clear the end of the jetty Tweed jumped up, opened a second door, ran up a flight of steps and was on the enclosed bridge. Marler was leaning through an open window on the starboard side, waving his hand to the left frantically. They were heading straight for a jagged spur of rock protruding into the channel, a spur which could rip a huge hole in the hull. He looked at Ben, who was already turning the ship to port. Peering over Marler's shoulders Tweed saw they slipped past the spur with a clearance of barely two feet. They emerged into the calm open sea.

'You can take over the wheel now, Marler,' shouted Ben. 'I have plotted the course from the map you sent me by courier. Just keep your ruddy eye on the compass.'

With Marler behind the wheel, Ben opened the door to the stateroom. Paula was sitting up, legs curled like a cat's, studying a marine report.

'You're supposed to be cooking!' Ben bellowed. 'Can't you find the ruddy galley?'

'Cooking is not in the contract,' Paula snapped without looking up. 'Shouldn't you be on the bridge, as captain of this old tub?'

Ben muttered an oath under his breath, slammed the door shut. On the bridge Tweed was standing close to Marler, staring ahead with fascination at the incredible vastness of the Atlantic. The *Tiger*'s port and starboard running lights were on. Ben saw him looking at them.

'Need 'em on in case we run into a Coastguard patrol. Further out I switches 'em off. Marler marked

Noak Island on the map he sent me. Talk about isolation – no airline flies near the place. And it's miles off
any shipping route.'

'Mr Neville Guile likes his privacy,' Tweed said to
himself.

Paula appeared and saw Harry, who had headed for
the bridge as soon as he came aboard. Typically, he sat
in a corner of the deck, knees bunched underneath
him. He had his bag open, which carried an amazing
mix of weapons and tools. He saw her watching him.
She settled down beside him.

'What are these secret weapons you keep so quiet
about? I might have to use one.'

'Put your gloves on. The devices are slippery.'

He shifted position so they were shielded from the
others. Out of the bag his gloved hand produced a
cylindrical object about a foot long with a switch
turned to green. Pushed forward it would point to red.

'For Pete's sake, and mine,' he whispered, 'don't
touch that switch. You do and this whole ship
explodes in flames, the sea boils. It's new, invented by
Mac down in the boffins' basement.'

'What's inside?' she whispered.

'Mix of high-explosive and firebomb. Got five of the
devils, all told. Don't know why Tweed wants 'em.'

Paula stood up, disappeared back into the stateroom. Tweed, on the bridge alongside Marler, was
puzzled.

'We're gliding over the sea as though it were a skating rink. But no engine sound.'

'Ben explained that,' Marler said, glancing at the compass and turning the wheel a fraction. 'The genius who built this vessel installed a special engine. If you listen carefully it makes no more sound than the purring of a cat. Another reason Noak won't know we're coming. Besides radar they'll have listening posts, I'm sure.'

Half an hour later someone was kicking the far side of the door from the stateroom. Tweed opened it and a glorious aroma of fish and chips entered his nostrils. Paula stood with a large plastic tray. It had depressions for servings and smaller ones for plastic cups of Evian water. As a matter of form she served the master of the ship first. Ben stared as though he couldn't believe it. Then, greedily, he grabbed a plate of fish and chips and a cup of water.

'*You!*' He gave her a great big toothy grin. 'You was windin' me up.'

'Shut up and eat,' she snapped back at him.

For a while there was no conversation on the bridge as they concentrated on eating. Paula had fetched her own meal on a separate tray. She whispered to Tweed, 'I haven't seen Bob Newman anywhere. Is he still in London?'

'No, he's one of my secret weapons,' Tweed whispered back. 'By now Guile will think he has identified my whole team. You, me, Harry and Marler. He won't know about Newman, who stays at one of those houses to let up the High Street. Don't know which one, don't want to know. He's wearing country clothes, a wide-brimmed straw hat and sunglasses. He

178

mooches around, posing as an architect with his nose in a book. But I'll bet he doesn't miss a thing.'

On the bridge by the wheel Ben had gripped Marler hard by the arm. He was peering ahead at a dark bulk with a red light shining high up. Noak Island.

'That's why I switched off all my lights,' Ben explained, 'but somehow they've spotted us.'

'Well, at least it was such a calm voyage,' Paula called out to introduce a note of optimism.

'Won't be if we ever return,' growled Ben. 'Forecast is for a real twister of a storm which should hit us halfway back.'

'I think I've entered the gap in the radar zone,' Marler said.

'You have,' Ben agreed. As he spoke there was an explosion to starboard.

'They know we're coming,' Tweed warned.

'No, they don't,' called out Ben. 'That was an old wartime mine deciding to welcome us. Never heard of one being this far out, though.'

They were close in to what appeared to be a giant chunk of rock. Ben turned on a searchlight and Tweed stared. He had expected another dangerous gulch entrance like the one at Seaward Cove they had left far behind. Instead in the glare of Ben's light was a wide harbour enclosed by high stone walls.

'This map is out of date,' Marler complained.

'Unless Neville Guile has blasted rock to create a favourable entrance for large vessels,' Tweed suggested.

'Like that one over there just going under,' Paula called out, and pointed.

Well over to port, away from Noak and the exploding mine, the hull of a large vessel which had turned turtle protruded briefly above the surface of the smooth sea. Tweed felt sure it was a huge tanker as it slid below the sea, leaving behind a small ripple of waves.

'That were a tanker going down,' Ben said. 'Big job. What's it doin' 'ere?'

'The tanker that pirates hijacked in the East,' Marler said with a flash of inspiration.

'I think you're right,' Tweed agreed. 'And no oil seeping out – because it was all pumped ashore first onto Noak. I don't like pirates but I'll bet their bodies, each with a bullet in the back of the head, are lying in the hold. After they'd helped pump the oil ashore. No witnesses is one of Neville Guise's rules of business. And look at that cliff.'

A monster of a black cliff sheered up from the harbour. By now Ben had brought *Tiger* alongside an inner wall of one of the stone jetties. He picked up a great coil of rope, threw it at Harry.

'Get ashore with that, tie it round one of those stone bollards, then make fast the stern. I'll be there with more rope.'

Harry jumped to his feet, grabbed the rope coil and followed Ben down a ladder from the bridge to the main deck. Leaping over the narrow gap onto the jetty, he wound lengths of rope round the stone bollard.

Paula had skipped down the ladder behind Ben. He placed a huge ugly-looking knife beside the rope on deck.

'What's the knife for?' she asked.

'Always curious, you ladies. If we have to run for it in a hurry, that knife can cut through the rope in seconds. Now I'm off to the stern. That Harry doesn't waste time.'

Paula shinned back up the ladder onto the bridge. Tweed was adjusting the glare light up the side of the precipitous cliff. At intervals he paused briefly. Paula saw a series of thick large rubber loops attached to the rock.

'What on earth—' she began.

'They attach a thick hose inside those loops and use a system to suck up the oil from the tanker berthed about where the *Tiger* is now.' He looked back to where Harry had appeared. 'Leather climbing boots for everyone except Ben. We've got to get to the top of this brute.'

Harry produced the boots from his capacious bag. On the soles were hard projections for clinging to ledges. At a fresh order from Tweed, Harry took out a backpack, slipped inside the torpedo-shaped weapons he had shown Paula – the firebombs. They began climbing, Tweed in the lead.

It was a difficult climb. The cliff face was almost vertical. Paula went up quickly, but tested her weight on every protruding spike of rock before trusting it. Harry was close behind her. She was about to turn to say something to him when Tweed's sharp whisper reached her as though he'd sensed what she was about to do.

'Nobody look down. That's a direct order. Look *up*!'

She hauled herself over the top before she realized how close to the summit she was. She pulled herself up the final few feet and sat still for a moment, breathing heavily. She looked down as Harry scrambled over with Marler close behind. Her mind began to swim with vertigo so she turned to look inland, amazed at the view.

A shallow slope led down no more than a hundred feet. She was staring at four vast container tanks, their roofs slightly curved. Beyond, the ground climbed steeply but at the far end of the island a long runway was laid out. A large plane stood at the takeoff end.

'You see,' said Tweed, seated close to her with the others very near, 'refineries and oil storage tanks. Contents – from that pirated tanker. Worth millions. Over on the far coast you can see a smaller fleet of tankers flying the Otranto flag. Neville planned on selling oil he'd not paid a penny for – to desperate countries who'd pay $100 a barrel for the stuff. Harry, I want all four of those oil tanks destroyed.'

'No sooner said than done,' Harry replied. 'I'll hike to the one furthest away.'

'Can I help you?' Paula suggested.

'Yes. By sitting there and not getting in my bloody way.'

They all knew he'd been deliberately rude to stop her coming with him on what could be a suicide mission.

'Maybe I—' began Marler.

'If you'll all shut your big mouths maybe I can concentrate,' Harry told them.

Then he was gone. Running, crouched, down the slope, he was about to pass the nearest tank. Then he saw the ladder curving up its side. It would give him height and he must now be near the more distant tank. He had his backpack turned to rest on his stomach. Arriving at the top he was closer to all four oil tanks than he'd expected. He extracted the first explosive firebomb.

Taking a deep breath he hurled it with all his strength at the most distant tank. His bomb landed dead centre on its curved surface. As he hurtled a fresh bomb at a nearer tank his first bomb detonated with a sinister crack. There was a dull explosion, then it blew apart, emanating a fireball. His second bomb was increasing the blinding blaze over the whole storage area.

He ran down the ladder, already feeling the heat from the fire. Running back up the slope, he paused, hurled two more bombs, one for each nearer tank. Then he ran like hell up the slope to join the others, gazing with disbelief at the spectacle. The flames from all four tanks had now merged into one massive inferno.

Paula had her binoculars pressed against her eyes.

They were aimed at the long runway with the large plane at the take-off point.

'They're all running for it. They're flying out. Plane's on the move. Guile has taken fright.'

'Didn't know how many of us there were,' Marler explained. 'It could have been a whole army.'

'Time to return to the ship,' Tweed decided. He grunted. 'It will be trickier descending that cliff than it was coming up. Be very careful.'

'Piece of cake,' said Harry. 'I need all your water bottles . . .'

Paula was puzzled. She watched as he withdrew from his pack a familiar object: a rope knotted at close intervals she had used to rescue MacBlade from the vertical tunnel under Black Gorse Moor. Producing a thick towel from the pack, he soaked it in water. After kicking a tall thick rock spike on the summit to test its strength he wrapped the towel round it a number of times, then tied the end of the rope over the wet towel.

'Now no danger of the rope fraying as we go down,' he explained. 'Everyone wears the best gloves they've got to ease the strain of their descent. Paula first. Then Tweed, with Marler behind him. I'll follow you lot.'

Paula already had her gloves on. Before she approached the rope she glanced inland. The big plane which would have Neville Guile aboard was already cruising down the runway prior to take-off. Mr Guile was a survivor.

Peering over the rim of the precipice, she saw

Harry's rope had reached the bottom. She bent down, grasped the first knot, continued to descend, not looking down. She used her feet to keep her body clear of the rock. Her feet suddenly touched the ground. She was startled at the speed of her descent. Looking up, she saw Tweed about to land beside her, then Marler. Finally, Harry seemed to descend like a trapeze artist.

'Get aboard the ship fast!' Tweed ordered.

Ben asked no questions, concentrating on backing his ship out of the harbour. Paula ran down the steps onto the foredeck. She looked up and Harry was watching her from an open window on the bridge. Gazing back to the base of the cliff, she stiffened. No guards? A massive North African had appeared, holding an automatic weapon. The huge figure was elevating the muzzle to sweep the bridge with one lethal burst of fire. He would kill them all, and he was grinning sadistically at the prospect of mass slaughter.

'Take this, Paula,' Harry yelled, almost falling from the window.

Reaching up, her gloved hand helped her to grasp the slippery surface. Switch forward – to red. She counted to three. While at school she had excelled at rounders. She hurled the missile, aiming for the large rock overhang he was sheltered beneath.

The firebomb detonated with such power it made the ship shudder. Paula had briefly closed her eyes against the brilliant flash, then opened them in time to see the immense tonnage of rock fall and bury the guard forever. She sighed with relief.

'Good shot,' Harry called down calmly. 'You get the prize.'

Tweed, who had witnessed the entire episode, had kept his mouth closed. He turned to Ben.

'Sea's like the proverbial millpond again. So a quiet voyage back to base.'

'Probably not,' Ben growled. 'Remember the forecast. About halfway back we'll have to fight a huge tornado-like storm . . .'

19

For more than half the return journey to Seaward Cove, the sea was so calm that again the *Tiger* seemed to glide over the surface. In the stateroom, Paula sat reading a shipping manual. On the couch opposite alongside the port side Tweed appeared to be fast asleep, eyes closed, head sunk on his chest. Paula was not deceived. She knew he was wide awake, ranging his mind over all that had happened in Hobartshire, listing the whole cast of the characters he had met, assessing them.

Marler appeared suddenly. He had been handling the wheel on the bridge, now briefly handed over to Ben.

'Sorry to interrupt,' he began. 'Better take a peek to the west.'

As he returned to the bridge the ship began to rock

and sway from side to side. Tweed stood up as Paula ran to peer through a window on the starboard side. They stood together for a moment, staring at the transformation. The moon cast a pale glow over the approaching violence. The ferocious storm was heading for them.

Paula grabbed her life jacket, slung from a hook, slipped it over her head, fastened the tie round her waist. Tweed already had donned his own kit. Ben appeared at the top of the steps.

'Big trouble,' he growled. 'Life jackets on.'

He stopped speaking when he saw they both were already equipped. The swaying movement was now so pronounced Ben had to hold on to hand-rails to haul himself back up to the bridge. At the top he yelled back at them over his shoulder.

'It's a *monster*!'

'That's right,' Paula yelled back, 'cheer us up . . .'

Standing next to Tweed and, like him, hanging on to a hand-rail above the couch, she had to admit Ben's description was hardly exaggerated. She gazed in awe as mountainous waves, reminding her of pictures she'd seen of the Himalayas, swept down a few hundred yards away. Massive waves collided with each other, sending up a smokescreen of surf concealing what was coming up behind them.

'The bridge,' Tweed snapped. 'Get up there now. I'll be behind you.'

It was a struggle to mount the staircase. Paula held tightly on to the same hand-rail. It was fortunate she'd taken this precaution. A mighty *whack*! told them a wave had hit the hull. As they reached the bridge Ben screamed at Marler manoeuvring the wheel.

'Don't let a wave hit us broadside on. We'll broach to—'

'Just shut up!' Marler shouted back.

Paula had every confidence in Marler's seamanship. On the rare occasions when he had time off he liked to sail off the south coast even in choppy weather. She glanced westward, sucked in her breath.

'A big one is coming,' she warned him.

'Thank you,' he said with a smile. 'I've just seen the brute.'

He was already turning the wheel and she thought she understood his tactics. He was going to ride the crest, use it to take them at speed nearer to home base. It was an odd sensation – to be carried forward by the power of the sea. It became very quiet suddenly.

She heard the sound of a large engine, looked up, gazed with disbelief at the huge plane descending towards them at speed, like the plane she'd seen taking off from Noak. It looked like an attack.

Harry had earlier adopted his usual position, crouched cross-legged in a corner of the deck. Now he leapt to his feet with binoculars hanging from a strap round his neck. Throwing open a window, he pressed the glasses briefly to his eyes. Then he shouted.

'Plane has one window open. Thug with an automatic weapon. He's going to spray this bridge with bullets!'

He ran, splay-legged to counter the deck tilt, across to Ben.

'Give me a Very light. Damn quick! Red if possible, if not, any colour. Move!'

Ben was already moving. Throwing open a cupboard door, he bent down, shoved his large hand inside. It emerged holding a metal object Paula only had a glimpse of. At one end of the squat instrument was a handle, at the other end a muzzle several inches in diameter. He passed it to Harry.

'It's *red* and loaded.' He told Harry. 'Specially made for me and other favoured customers by an engineer pal down the coast. Costs a small fortune.'

He was now speaking to Marler. Harry only heard the first few words. Once he had the Very light in his hand he rushed to the open window. The huge plane seemed only yards above them but that was an optical illusion.

Resting both arms on the ledge of the open window – for stability – Harry aimed the Very light at the plane's port engine. He pressed the trigger. At that moment the *Tiger* rolled. The missile shot upwards, exploded in a blinding glare below the fuselage. Harry swore to himself but the explosion frightened the pilot. Had the Very been sucked inside the engine as it detonated the plane would have dived into the maelstrom.

Panicking, the pilot elevated his machine to a high altitude and flew off, heading for the coast. Paula sighed with relief. Tweed simply shrugged as he asked Ben the question.

'Ben, I presume that plane is flying off to land at Heathrow or London's City Airport?'

'Don't think so. My guess is it will land at the private airfield about three miles east of the ridge overlooking Seaward Cove.'

'Not far away, then. Can you see this airfield from the ridge summit?'

'No,' Ben told him. 'It's hidden behind another ridge. Below my ridge there's a road to London and a turning off to this airfield. Funny thing. My ridge this side is as solid as Everest – but on the other side the surface is loose shale. One day it will break loose; send an avalanche down onto that road.'

'Tell me,' Tweed persisted, 'who owns the airfield?'

It was Marler who answered. He'd had a quiet stretch across a peculiar area of uncannily quiet water. More like a lake than the sea.

'It's owned,' he explained, 'by an obscure company with a strange name.' He looked at Paula. 'Excuse my Latin, which will make you wince. Name of company is Veni, Vidi, Vici . . .'

'You pronounced that very well,' said Paula, who had been good at Latin at school.

'What does it mean?' Tweed asked.

'It's the opening sentence of Julius Caesar's *Gallic Wars*,' she told him. 'Translated it means "I came. I saw. I conquered."'

'Known for short as the VVV Corp,' Marler added.

'Sounds like a good motto for our Mr Neville Guile,' Tweed commented.

'While you lot have been chattering,' Ben said in his fiercest growl, 'you might look at what's coming for us to starboard. Marler, like me to take over from you? Had a long stint.'

'It's OK, Ben,' Marler assured him. 'I'll take her into the cove.'

Secretly, Ben was relieved. Marler was the younger man. He had great strength in his arms and a quick reflex in turning the wheel. Knowing what was coming, Ben was doubly thankful as he joined Tweed and Paula, their hands gripping the handrail.

'The Devil comes in after the quiet stretch of water we've just crossed,' he said quietly.

Paula was staring, fixated, to the west. She had never seen anything like it. About half a mile wide, the immense wave appeared to be moving slowly, but this was an illusion. Already higher than the top of the ship's funnel, it was sucking up smaller waves, swelling itself to even greater size as it rolled closer and closer. Paula became aware Marler was turning their ship through a hundred and eighty degrees.

He was going to try and ride the crest of this giant. Could he possibly make it? It would be a miracle if he managed it. She turned to Tweed.

'How much further to Seaward Cove?'

'Not much,' he replied cheerfully. 'You can see the red light perched above the prawn workshop.'

She looked ahead, clenched her fists inside her pockets. The red light which came on at intervals for five minutes was no more than a distant pinpoint. The foredeck of the ship was climbing now. The deadly self-inflating wave had reached them. She tensed for the steep drop deep down into the ocean which would precede its mounting of the side beyond. She had a premonition that once the *Tiger* started descending it would continue plunging until the forepart was smashed to pulp as the entire vessel settled deep down in its watery grave.

'Marler is a master seaman,' Tweed said casually.

'*What?*'

'He is riding the crest of that giant wave, has reduced speed to coincide with it. It's carrying us home.'

Paula looked again at the red light above Seaward Cove. The light above the prawn workshop was much larger. They were so close now to the coast. Her only doubt was what would happen when the wave reached the narrow harbour. Ben, watching her, must have sensed her anxiety.

'We are now entering one of those strange lakes of calm we saw earlier. The wave is vanishing.'

'It is?' she called back, trying to sound confident.

Then, peering out of a window across the foredeck, she saw – *felt* – *Tiger* descending gently but steadily. The wave was subsiding. Soon its surface was on a level with the harbour wall.

She climbed down the steps into the stateroom. Officially, if asked, she was clearing up the stateroom. The truth was she had had enough. She didn't want to watch them passing through the snake-like entrance, evading the brutal spars of rock by two feet or less. The ship stopped suddenly and she knew they were mooring to the jetty. She ran up the steps.

Harry, onshore, had just completed tying the rope to the stern bollard. She joined Tweed and the others on the jetty. The weird and sombre light of dawn was illuminating the summit of the eastern ridge. Ben, standing close to his house, cupped both hands and bellowed.

'I'll be gettin' breakfast. A large omelette and crispy bacon.'

'A two-egg omelette for me,' Harry bellowed back.

'So now we can have a quiet day,' Paula mused aloud.

'I wouldn't count on that,' Tweed warned. 'No, I wouldn't . . .'

20

They had finished a large well-cooked breakfast, seated round an oblong table with a well-scrubbed surface covered with a thick white cloth. All was peace and quiet.

It was daylight, another brilliant day. The sun shone on the calm sea, creating sparkling reflections like a spread of diamonds. Only Tweed sat very still looking serious. Ben spoke to him.

'You'll have to drive back along the same road you came in on. There's another track to the west I drive over on my Land Rover for food and supplies. No use to you – it ends at a large village. So you have to use the way you came in on, no matter where you're heading for.'

'London, straight to Finden Square,' Tweed said grimly.

Paula stared at him. By the tone of his voice she knew they had reached their first climax. It was a development she had seen before. Tweed had turned aggressive, in an attacking mood. The initiative had passed into his hands.

'The point I'm making,' Ben growled, 'was you drive back at a slow pace until you've passed the turn-off to that airfield. It is essential.'

'Why?' demanded Marler.

'If you listen you'll know why,' Ben growled again. 'My side of that high ridge to the east of here is solid, has stood like that since Stonehenge. The other side of the ridge is unstable. It's shale and one day immense tons will sweep down the ridge as a minor avalanche. Probably only stop when it's heaped up across the road or the barren fields beyond. Police put up warning signs but some crazy kids pulled the signs down then dumped them into the sea. In any case, that road only leads to a deserted beach unless you turn off to come to me.'

'Sounds a potential hazard,' Tweed commented.

'Not if you *crawl*,' warned Ben, 'until the airfield turn-off. Funny thing is, the fifty yards of ground at the top of the summit is hard immovable rock. But you *crawl*,' he repeated.

'Heard you the first time, Ben,' Marler said off-handedly.

'And I heard you coming in that Maserati,' Ben snapped.

They all stood up, gathered round Ben, thanked

him for all his help. Tweed put a hand on his shoulder.

'Sorry it was such a murderous nerve-racking trip. We are all so grateful.'

'Get off! The sea has its moods and I knows 'em.'

They travelled as they had come. Paula jumped into the passenger seat of the Maserati as Marler slipped in behind the wheel. Harry sat alongside Tweed, who took the wheel of the Audi, his mobile in one hand. They took off along the same road, which rounded the end of the ridge for a short distance with the sea close to their right, then descended for minutes onto the road below the ridge Ben had warned them about. Paula found an irresistible urge to look up to the summit. She was relieved that Marler was holding his speed to 25 m.p.h. or less. Then she stared, used her binoculars.

'There's someone on the hard rock at the top, looked like one of these North Africans. Dark face, cloth wrapped round his forehead . . .'

She heard a distant cracking sound, then another further along. At that moment the mobile buzzed. Marler snatched it up. He listened for a moment. His reply bothered Paula.

'OK, Harry. Thought so. I'm ramming my foot down. Could be a close-run thing for us . . .

'Neville Guile's gangsters are on the hard rock up there. They're throwing grenades to start the shale moving. It is. They're going to crush us before we reach safety!'

As he spoke he pressed his foot hard on the accelerator. They were racing as though at Le Mans. Glancing in the rear-view mirror Paula saw Tweed was only yards behind them, moving at the same manic speed. They swung round narrow bends, recovered, sped on.

Horrified, she gazed at the mountainous slope of the ridge. The whole surface was on the move. The shale had gathered into incredibly fast-moving waves, riding higher and higher as it thundered down the slope, sending down a thunderous roar, now over six feet high along the whole unstable slope. She gazed ahead and the turn-off to the airfield seemed miles ahead. They weren't going to make it. They'd end up buried in the pulverized metal of their vehicles.

She glanced at Marler. His expression was calm, concentrated. Ahead was a long straight stretch of road. Marler pressed his foot down hard. They were travelling at well over ninety miles an hour. She checked the rear-view mirror. The Audi was hurtling forward at the same speed. She forced herself to look at the rapidly advancing wall. It seemed almost on top of them, a mixture of large rocks 'cemented' together with the bloody shale. And still the turn-off to the airfield, to safety, seemed miles away. Paula had never been so frightened but she compelled herself to conceal her fear as the thunder of the landslide became almost deafening.

To take her mind off the hideous approaching landslide, Paula looked to her right. She had the same
impression of the 'scenery' as she had when they had
driven to Seaward Cove. Many areas of Somerset and
Devon were delightful and beautiful. This was not one
of them.

This was a desert of rock and derelict fields, so
barren and with nothing green anywhere that she was
vaguely reminded of the Mojave Desert in America.
No hotels, not even a house. She looked away,
checked the landslide.

It was close to overwhelming the road. Marler
glanced at her with a dry smile.

'OK, Paula?'

She managed to wink at him. He grinned back,
swiftly stared back at the straight road. His foot was
still pressed fully down and the car shuddered under
the pressure. Looking again in the rear-view mirror
she saw Tweed waving to her with a wide smile. He
looked so cool and calm.

Ahead of them a large round rock rolled across
the road. It told her the avalanche was nearly on
top of them. Then she leaned forward, tense.
They had nearly reached the turn-off to the airfield.
She couldn't believe it. As they swept past it she
checked the rear-view mirror once more, scared for
Tweed. She sagged as she saw the Audi pass the
turn-off.

Looking back behind the Audi she saw no sign of
the road – only the seven-foot-high tumble of rock and

199

shale that covered it. The tension slowly drained out of her as Marler slowed to a normal speed.

'Where to next?' she wondered, trying to recall something said earlier. Park Crescent would be my choice, she thought.

21

They were still in the wilds when Marler received a message from Tweed. Slipping his mobile into his pocket, he grinned at Paula.

'I'm pulling in at that layby ahead of us. Tweed will join us there. Our next destination is Finden Square, the lion's den.'

'Why?' demanded Paula.

'Here is Tweed. You rejoin him in the Audi. Harry will be travelling with me.'

'OK, Paula,' said Tweed as he appeared, opening the door for her. 'I'll take over the lead from now on,' he told Marler.

'You must be mad,' Paula snapped as she settled beside Tweed in the Audi. 'He'll be expecting you at Finden – with an army of thugs.'

'I've changed my mind. We're heading straight back

to Hobartshire. I'll inform Marler in a moment. As in the past, I had a surge of fury, and misjudgement, when I thought that landslide was going to kill you.'

'You'd have been killed too,' she pointed out.

'Goes with the territory where I'm concerned.' He used her mobile to tell Marler of the change of destination. 'He also likes the idea. Our main task is still to identify the murderer.'

'Any narrowing of the list of suspects?' she enquired.

'Possibly. A motive has appeared but it may not be right.'

Paula took a last look at the bleak inland landscape. She was so looking forward to getting away from the treacherous sea. To be revelling in the greenery of Hobartshire, the strange old town of Gunners Gorge.

It was mid-morning and still May. The sun shone out of a blue sky. The temperature indicator inside the car registered 70°F in the open. Perfect – Paula settled down to enjoy the ride as they entered green countryside with rolling slopes and passed under arcades of dense trees in full leaf creating a boulevard-like atmosphere. Then the mobile buzzed. Tweed grabbed it.

'Tweed here. Bob! Great to hear from you. *What*? Accident? Has he survived? Thank heavens for that. We're on our way to you from Seaward Cove. Expect our arrival about dusk. OK. Meet you inside the garage at the Nag's Head. Watch your back.'

'Something has happened?' asked Paula.

'An attempt was made to kill Lord Bullerton this morning.'

'Neville Guile,' she said.

'Doubt that. They were still doing business together.'

'Maybe they'd completed their business, so Guile—'

'Maybe, maybe, maybe,' Tweed responded irritably. His voice changed to normal. 'Now there could be a motive there. I think the fog is clearing over these mass murders. Must let Marler and Harry know.'

He spoke briefly on the mobile, knowing the quick-witted Marler would grasp the situation when told in a few words.

Then he concentrated on his driving. Half his mind was on this startling new development. Paula tapped his arm gently.

'You're driving much faster. Only just under the speed limit . . .'

'I know the speed limit,' he rapped back.

'I'm sure you do.' Paula changed the subject. 'I really am looking forward to seeing Bob again.'

'So am I. I suspect he may have accumulated a whole load of information as to what is really going on up there. Something is. I said earlier I believe it's something big. I'm more than ever convinced about that.'

'Bob won't have wasted his time. The energy of the man is phenomenal.'

'Paula . . .' He looked at her and smiled. 'I apologize for my recent irritability. An attack on Bullerton is the last thing I expected.'

'You've been under tremendous pressure. Please forget the apology. Not necessary. You took a wise decision to return to Hobartshire.'

'We could be walking into a dangerous situation,' he warned.

'Situation normal,' she replied calmly.

It was dusk when they arrived at the Nag's Head and drove slowly into the garage. Newman appeared from behind Harry's grey Fiat. For a moment Paula didn't recognize him. He was wearing khaki drill, a straw hat, brim pulled well down over his face, and dark glasses. He removed hat and glasses and came forward to hug her.

'Good to see you,' Tweed called out, still seated behind the wheel of the Audi. 'What do you advise as our immediate objective?'

'Drive with Paula and Harry to Hobart House right now. I can talk when you get back. Suggest dinner in your suite.'

Driving to Hobart House, Paula found it strange to be back in familiar surroundings. She sat beside Tweed who was behind the wheel. Harry occupied the rear of the Audi. Approaching the turn-off lane at the nearest end of the Village, he leaned forward.

'I don't believe it. Mrs Grout is scrubbing her steps again.'

'Maybe a cat with muddy paws climbed them,' Paula joked.

'Drop me off close to that hole in the hedge,' Harry requested. 'Anyone pursuing you up that slope will get a bullet closer to his legs than he'll like.'

When they drove on down to Hobart House it was pitch black. The moon was obscured by a low bank of dark clouds. Every light in the residence was on.

The front door was opened by Lance. Wearing a pale grey blazer and cream trousers, he looked as smart as he always did. His expression was one of relief when he saw them under the glow of the porch lantern.

'Am I glad to see the two of you. Something awful has happened.'

'How is your father?' Tweed asked as they entered the hall.

'Lucky to be alive. Who would do such a thing? Father is in his study, working on some papers. He's amazing. The doctor has been, checked him over. No bones broken and no injury to the muscular system. I'll take you to him.'

'Hold it a second,' Tweed ordered. 'When did this happen? In the early morning? I see. Now, who was in the house at the time?'

'Let's sec.' Lance frowned. 'I was here, so were Margot and Sable – in their rooms. Mrs Shipton was here – gets in to her kitchen where she is now at crack of dawn. To deal with the girl staff from the town, and they'd gone by then. I think that's the lot. No, the stable staff were in their stables.' He smiled ruefully. 'Dawn cracks when it sees them coming.'

'What was the nature of the so-called accident?'

'My father couldn't sleep, so he got up earlier than usual to take his morning ride before breakfast. Apparently found his horse, Fairlight, already saddled for him. Jumps on it, goes riding along the course. Was just about to go over a high hurdle when his saddle tips sideways, throws him off. Luckily they hadn't mown the side grass yet, which broke his fall.'

'Who saddles his horse?'

'Jacko, chief stable lad.'

'Thank you. We'd like to see your father now.'

Lance led the way to the study. Opening the door, he called out, 'Company which you'll welcome!'

As they walked into the spacious room, Lord Bullerton was at a desk pushed against the wall. Its surface was covered with papers. Lord Bullerton's bulk was settled in a tall Queen Anne straight-backed chair. What happened next startled Tweed.

Bullerton turned sideways, saw his visitors, leapt up and stomped steadily towards them. His hand was outstretched, his tread normal.

'Welcome, Tweed, and you too, Paula. I couldn't have expected two more interesting visitors at this time of night. I suggest you both celebrate with me over double Scotches.'

He indicated a large glass on the desk. It was already half empty.

'Paula,' he continued vigorously, 'come and join me on the couch. You're looking more beautiful than ever.'

'I hear you've had a bad so-called accident,' said Tweed, 'being tipped off your horse close to a high hurdle.'

'When you ride a lot, as I do, these things happen.' Bullerton finished off his Scotch, poured himself another. 'No point in fussing.'

'This was a carefully planned attempt . . .' Tweed paused, 'and I don't think you've grasped it yet – to murder you.'

'Oh, come off it, Tweed.'

'I've had a lot of experience with crime. Somebody attempted to murder you,' he repeated in a harsh voice, 'and make it look like an accident.'

At last it had hit home. Bullerton walked back and sagged into his chair. Paula thought his earlier ruddy complexion had turned pale. He lifted his refilled glass, put it down without drinking.

'Who would want to do a thing like that?' he asked.

'I have several motives in mind – and several suspects . . .'

He stopped speaking as the door was pushed open and Harry appeared. Paula had been wondering where he was. He was holding on to a young man by twisting his arm behind his back. In his late teens or very early twenties, Paula estimated. His thick black hair was ruffled and he wore a well-worn dark suit.

'This is Jacko,' Harry announced. 'Found him very anxious to get away from the stable.'

'Going to see my girl friend,' Jacko burbled. 'She cuts up rough if I'm late.'

'You've heard about the so-called accident,' Tweed interrupted grimly. 'Did you saddle the horse for Lord Bullerton today as usual?'

'No, sir . . . I didn't . . . His Lordship had never arrived so early before . . . I was appalled when I heard what happened.'

'So appalled,' Harry rasped, still holding Jacko's arm, 'you made your first priority scooting away from here.'

'She's special . . .' the lean handler began.

'They all are. Until you meet—'

'Harry,' Tweed intervened again, 'you can let go of his arm. Very roughly he addressed Jacko. 'Who else was with you to confirm your story? Where were you?'

'No one, sir. I was in the adjoining barn, changing into my working kit. And I didn't see anyone else. It was very early.'

'Harry,' Tweed ordered, 'see him off the premises – first get his address.'

Bullerton had a sip of his scotch. He appeared to have calmed down as he spoke emphatically.

'I'd trust Jacko with my life.'

'Maybe you did,' Tweed said quietly. 'I think you should see this instruction from a Yard commander. It gives me full authority to search this house from roof to cellar.'

'I don't need to see it – after what happened today. Tear the place to pieces. Can't imagine what you'll find. Oh, at the very back of the brush cupboard in the kitchen there is a secret panel. You just push the right-hand side. My personal documents are inside. Read what you want.'

'Who in this house is a good rider?' Tweed enquired.

'All of them. Lance, Sable, Margot and Mrs Shipton. She is a wizard on a horse.'

'Where will I find Mrs Shipton now?'

'In her lair, in the kitchen . . .'

Tweed tapped lightly on the closed kitchen door. Nothing. He tapped a little louder.

'Go drop off a cliff,' Mrs Shipton's strong voice barked. 'I won't have anyone in here, whoever you are!'

Tweed opened the door quietly. Mrs Shipton stood at the far end of her work table. She had a wide aluminium bowl close to her together with a smaller variety of dishes filled with different ingredients.

'Get out, both of you!' she stormed.

Tweed was holding a document he had unfolded. He waved it at her. Wearing a spotless apron, Mrs Shipton glared at him.

'And what might that be?'

'An authority signed by a Yard commander giving permission for us to search the whole house. Any resistance is a criminal offence.'

'You mean you propose to search my bedroom?' she demanded, her hands on her hips.

'If that becomes necessary I shall not venture inside. Paula alone will enter.'

'You do realize why I'm working this late?' she snapped.

Colin Forbes

'No idea.'

'Because at this hour His Lordship has decided he'd like me to make his favourite dish. A soufflé.'

'He's had a nasty shock today,' Paula said quietly.

'Were you here when it happened?' Tweed demanded, seizing on the opening.

'I suppose I must have been.' Mrs Shipton sat down in a wicker chair. 'He got up exceptionally early I gather for a pre-breakfast ride. Never known him up so early.'

'Anyone else about at that hour?'

'Only the hiker.'

'What was he doing here? Can you describe him, please.'

'About five feet eight tall. Very well dressed, with a pack on his back. Lean and agile. The odd thing was his complexion – very pale. Had a slightly crooked nose. Very polite. Needed a glass of water. I took him through into here, he drank all the water.'

Paula turned her back on Mrs Shipton and mouthed 'Lepard' to Tweed. The description perfectly matched Harry's description of the villain.

'Which route did he follow when he left?' Tweed asked.

'Very considerate. Said he didn't want to risk leaving mud from his boots on our beautiful carpets. Was there a more direct way out of the kitchen? I pointed him through the back door along that footpath.'

'Does that lead anywhere near the barn where Lord Bullerton mounted his horse before his accident?'

210

'Yes, it does. Can't see it from here.'

'Would this be a few minutes before Lord Bullerton went to the barn?'

'I've no damned idea.' Her patience snapped as Tweed, with latex gloves on, opened a tall door, realized it was the broom cupboard with neatly stacked equipment hung by string from hooks on both side walls. 'Don't you go messing that up,' shrieked Mrs Shipton, 'I'm an organized woman and—'

Tweed, shining a powerful torch and now deep inside, heard her switching her tirade on Paula, who was opening several wall cupboards containing expensive crockery. He passed a five-foot-tall metal drum, from the top of which protruded a collection of well-used brushes and mops. Reaching the back wall of white panels, he pressed the right-hand side hard. It swung inward on a central metal pivot. Inside was a cardboard roll, which he extracted.

By the light of his torch he read the legal document quickly. He raised his eyebrows in surprise, refolded the document, slid it back inside the tube, replaced the protective cap and tucked it under his arm.

On his way to the exit he noticed again the drum crammed with used brushes and mops. It was then he noticed a long green rod shoved between them. Its handle was rusted. Still wearing the gloves, he eased the whole handle out. At the working end were remnants of an ancient mop. His expression became grim.

Walking back into the kitchen, he closed the door. Paula was just closing the last of the cupboards she had searched. She smiled at Tweed, then noticed his expression.

'Find any treasures?' she asked quietly.

'Have you a long enough evidence envelope for this handle?'

'Might have. Let me look in my briefcase.'

In no time she hauled out an envelope folded several times. Extending it, she held it out to Tweed, who slipped the green handle inside. She sealed the top, wrote the date and place on a card attached to the envelope's mouth.

'What do you want that old thing for?' Mrs Shipton demanded. 'Where did you get it?'

'I have never seen such a neat and well-organized kitchen,' Paula told Mrs Shipton when Tweed didn't reply. 'You are such a well-organized person. I know I'm repeating myself but I'm so impressed.'

'Time we left,' Tweed said abruptly, heading for the door leading to the hall. 'Sorry to disturb you, Mrs Shipton.'

Lance met them in the hall. As usual, his eyes roamed over Paula.

'Two odd visitors have arrived to see Father,' he told them. 'Sable, the idiot, answered the door, took them straight to the study. She rushed past me to her room. I asked her who they were. "No idea," she snapped.'

'Did you hear a word either of them said?'

'I was on the landing. They never said a word. One was incredibly tall and thin. He—'

Tweed walked fast across the hall, took hold of the

study door, threw it open and entered. Paula was at his heels.

Lord Bullerton was seated at his desk, looking very aggressive. Seated facing him on a couch were Neville Guile and Lepard.

22

Lord Bullerton looked up. Tweed thought he detected relief in his expression. He raised a clenched fist, crashed it down on his desk.

'Tweed, this man wants me to sell him Black Gorse Moor. I'm not going to do it for any price.'

'A million pounds is a lot of money,' Guile sneered.

'He has also,' Bullerton continued, 'threatened me if I refuse. Look at the thug he's brought with him.'

'I'm a professional carpenter.'

'Look,' Bullerton exploded, 'at his right leg! Just lift the trouser.'

Tweed had already observed the large holster not exposed. In it was sheathed a huge wide-bladed knife. Paula, who had also seen it, had sidled round behind Lepard. In her hand she held the .32 Browning slipped out of her own leg holster.

Close behind Lepard, she pressed the muzzle hard against the back of his neck. He stiffened. He knew what that meant.

'It would be murder,' he said unconvincingly. 'You'd spend a bad twelve years in Holloway.'

'Don't think so,' said Paula in a hard bitter tone. 'Not with two impeccable witnesses to confirm you were attacking Lord Bullerton.'

'Take it easy,' Guile told Lepard.

'I never do.'

'That's an order I'm giving you,' Guile said in his cut-glass voice.

He was disturbed by the hard tone of Paula's voice. Time to quieten down a dangerous situation.

'Now,' began Paula, talking to Lepard, 'you will do exactly what I tell you. Any tricks and my trigger finger is itchy. Bend slowly forward, undo the straps on your holster. Don't touch that knife.'

Lepard slowly bent down. As he did so Paula kept the Browning's muzzle pressed against his neck. He unfastened the straps, his face a picture of fury. To be humiliated by a woman. He held holster and knife well away from himself.

'Now put it on that table by your side,' Paula ordered. 'I want you to use your elbow to push the whole thing way over that table. That's right. You can sit up straight now.' She looked at Tweed, spoke again to Lepard. 'Don't forget my gun will be inches from your head.'

Tweed stepped forward, hands thrust deep inside his coat. He stared grimly at the billionaire.

'Guile, I'm warning you not to visit Hobart House. Never again slip into the grounds of his property. If you do I'll arrest you at once. You'll be transported in a police car to the Yard, held there while I phone Chief Inspector Loriot of the DST in Paris, ask him to send for your immediate extradition to France. I gather he wishes to interrogate you about certain of your activities in Europe. Now, both of you, leave.'

As he stood up Paula saw Guile stare at Tweed with a look of venom she'd never seen on another human being's face. Without a word he walked into the hall through the doorway Tweed had opened, followed by Lepard with Paula holding her gun close behind him.

Margot, close to the front door, unlocked, opened it. They walked out, down the steps towards their parked Citroën.

'I gather they're not wanted on the voyage,' Margot said wittily. She turned to a bank of switches, pressed two. The hall was plunged into darkness, but outside the terrace and beyond were illuminated with searchlight-like glares.

'Just to make sure they leave,' Margot said with a smile. 'I must get back to my room and homework, if you'll excuse me . . .'

She reached the top landing and bumped into Lance, who was on his way from his room. He squeezed her arm, ran down the staircase and across the hall to Tweed and Paula.

'Who were those peculiar people?' he asked. 'They never said a word.'

'Some businessmen who came to coax a loan from your father. He refused.'

'He's always being pestered by people who want money. Often over the phone.'

'Excuse me,' Tweed said, 'I have a private call to make.'

In a distant corner, dark despite the lights Margot had turned on again before she left, he pressed Harry's number.

'That you, Harry? Good. Where are you?'

'In a hole in a hedge, watching a Citroën approach from the mansion.'

'Inside are Neville Guile and his henchman, Lepard. They should drive along the lane. I want to make sure they leave. Paula and I will soon be driving up that way. Will pick you up. At the end of the lane the Citroën will turn left for the London road.'

'Got my car parked in a field. See you.'

Tweed returned to where Lance and Paula were chatting amiably.

'I really didn't like the look of the tall one with the cut-glass voice. Slithers when he walks.'

'Good metaphor,' Tweed said with a smile. 'He's a snake.'

'Hadn't we better get back and make sure Lord Bullerton is all right?' Paula suggested firmly.

Lance ran back up the stairs, As Tweed passed a wall of bookcases he paused, felt behind the wide gap behind them, took out the cardboard roll he'd found at the back of the brush cupboard in the kitchen. Paula looked puzzled.

'Why didn't we take that to Lord Bullerton earlier?'

She'd been shown it on their way from kitchen to hall. A lightning-quick reader, she had memorised its contents.

'Not in front of other people. Good job I didn't, considering who his visitors were.'

Entering the study, they found Bullerton seated again behind his desk. He was drinking the last of a double Scotch and another glass was waiting for him on the desk. He waved his glass to them.

'Cheers! And I can't thank you both so much for protecting me.'

Tweed sat down close to him, hammered the roll on the desk.

'What is all this about? You must tell me. It could be a link with my murder investigation.'

'Thought you'd find it. Has Paula also read it? Good. It is a legal document drawn up by Fingle, local solicitor. On Neville Guile's instructions. He has signed it, I have not and won't.'

'You'd be selling the whole of Black Gorse Moor and all the geological material beneath it for a million,' said Paula. 'A cool million pounds,' she repeated. 'What could be worth money like that?'

'No idea,' Bullerton told her. 'But if a crook like Neville Guile offers that much whatever it is has to be worth ten or twenty times as much. Only Archie

MacBlade could tell you. He wants to meet you for a late supper at the Nag's Head.'

'But I thought Hartland Trent and now, presumably his heirs, had a seventy per cent holding in the moor,' Tweed insisted.

'That was so. Emphasis on past tense. Guile moves fast when a fortune is at stake. I raised the Trent issue with him. He gave that awful giggle of his. He'd used Fingle first to rush through the transfer of Hartland's estate to his son, Barton. Then he offers the twenty-year-old Barton – not too bright – seven thousand pounds for the holding.'

'The robber baron,' Paula exclaimed.

'Young Barton tells Guile he needs ten thousand pounds. He has a pal with a car he's mad to buy. After haggling Guile, apparently reluctantly, agrees to pay ten thousand. Guile has the sale document with him and Barton signs with two neighbours as witnesses. Guile showed me the document.'

'But without your signature on this document I brought in he has nothing.'

'Nothing.'

'If you don't mind,' Tweed said, standing up, 'I'm anxious to talk to Archie . . .'

Minutes later Tweed, with Paula by his side, was driving the Audi, slowly along the hedge-lined lane. Harry appeared in his headlights, waving.

'Neville Guile didn't take the left turn towards London,' he reported tersely. 'He took the right-hand turn heading for Gunners Gorge.'

'Wait here,' Tweed ordered. 'Your job – guard Lord Bullerton.'

'So we haven't seen the last of Mr Guile,' Paula mused.

'Never mind. We're about to learn the secret of Black Gorse Moor.'

23

Alighting from the Audi inside the garage they met Marler, just emerging from the hotel. He gave them both a mock salute.

'I've been on the prowl, as Harry would say. Checking on the suspects,' he drawled. 'Falkirk, famous private detective, is in his room. On same floor as yours, Tweed. Archie MacBlade is having a drink in the Silver Room. See you . . .'

'The Silver Room?' queried Tweed. 'How many bars in this place?'

'In order of low to high –' Paula counted on her fingers – 'a saloon bar, only really patronized in the evening. Public bar, more popular with local workmen. Top of the tree, the luxurious Silver Room with prices to match.'

'I see. Let's get up to my suite. I need to think about

what happened at Hobart House. May ask you to take notes . . .'

He was on the landing, heading for his suite, when Falkirk walked towards them on his way out. He nodded to Paula. She had sensed that Tweed's normally exceptional energy had reached a ferocious pitch. He was in no mood to put up with nonsense from anyone. He stood in front of Falkirk, blocking his exit.

'A word with you, Falkirk. In my suite.'

'Not convenient, old boy. I am just—'

'I mean *now*!'

'Not convenient.'

Tweed grabbed him tightly by the collar with one hand, with the other he handed Paula the key to his suite. She ran to open his door. He was pushing Falkirk backwards along the corridor, into his suite and across the room, where he threw him bodily into an armchair backed against the wall. Falkirk leapt up instantly, grabbed Tweed's throat and started to strangle him. Paula stood by. She knew Tweed would want to sort this out himself. With both hands he grasped Falkirk's arms above the elbows, pressed both hands against certain nerves. Pain appeared on Falkirk's face. He released his hands from Tweed's throat and was hurled back into the armchair. Again he leapt up, right legs raised to kick his opponent in the crotch. Tweed avoided the vicious kick, moved to one side, grasped Falkirk by the shoulders and threw him with some force against the wall. Paula heard his head contact the wall. Falkirk's eyes glazed over as he slid down.

Tweed bent down. He checked the carotid artery, then his pulse. He spoke to Paula over his shoulder.

'Conscious, just stunned. Could you get me a glass of water?'

Paula ran to the fridge. From a carafe she poured a large glass, handed it to Tweed. By now he had hoisted Falkirk off the floor and dropped him back into the armchair. He handed the glass to Falkirk, who was sagged against the chair's back.

'You sip this slowly,' Tweed ordered. 'After six sips you can drink a modest amount.'

Falkirk smiled wanly after drinking most of the glass, gazing at Tweed.

'They said you were tough. By George, they were right. What's now?' he asked in a normal voice.

Tweed carried a hard-backed chair close to Falkirk. He turned it round, sat with both arms resting on the top in front of him, his voice harsh during the interrogation.

'Who hired you?'

'Lizbeth Mandeville, younger sister of the two murdered women.'

'You were the first person she approached?'

'No, she'd called the Yard.'

'Where from?'

'She's smart. From a public phone box.'

'What did Lizbeth say to them?'

'That there were two murdered mutilated women

lying outside on the steps of a house at the end of Lynton Avenue.'

'What was their reaction?'

'Bloody terrible. The very rough policeman who answered asked for her name, address and where she was calling from.'

She got Reedbeck, Paula said to herself.

'She was furious, demanded when they were sending a patrol car. The rough-mannered policeman simply repeated his questions. She slammed the phone down on him. In the box she noticed a booklet someone had left listing private detectives. She took it home. For some weird reason she liked the name of my firm, called me. I buzzed straight over to her, middle of the night.'

'First you checked the corpses?'

'I did not. Lizbeth sounded scared out of her wits. We had an arrangement – at her suggestion. I wore a red tie and had a folded newspaper under my left arm. Lizbeth is smart. Re. corpses, I did see the one on the steps of the next-door house. Horrible. Her face was destroyed. Must be a sadist . . .'

'Or there could be another motive,' Tweed said. 'Go on. What happened next?'

'Rolls-Royce turns up, hardly moving when it passes the corpse. Checked the plate number later. Private car owned by Neville Guile, the billionaire. Bit weird. He had the tinted window down, was peering out towards the corpse. Then he cruises off round the corner where later I found the other sister mangled.'

'Then what?'

'Two police cars turn up. One with the technicians, the other with Speedy Reedbeck – only two hours after Lizbeth's call.'

'After that?'

'You know. I was falsely arrested by Reedbeck.'

'What I don't yet know,' Tweed continued in the same aggressive manner, 'is how you knew about Hobartshire.'

'Lizbeth told me all about where she had been brought up. She refused point blank to go up here with me. The prospect made her tremble. She thinks the murderer lives there.'

'All your story –' Tweed stood up – 'can be checked out with Lizbeth, who is now travelling north to Hobartshire under armed guard.'

'Is that wise?' queried Falkirk prior to leaving.

'I'll decide what is wise. I may have to see you later.'

'Can't decide what I need first,' their visitor remarked as Paula opened the door. 'A good hot bath or a really strong Scotch.'

'The bath first,' Paula told him firmly. 'His story appeared to fit the facts precisely,' she remarked after relocking the door.

'I've decided we'll have our planned supper with Archie MacBlade in the dining room. It's claustrophobic up here.'

Paula phoned the dining room for a quiet table. Then she got through to Archie, who accepted with enthusiasm. As she put down the phone she noticed Tweed was staring into the distance.

'What is it?' she asked.

'Your remark about Falkirk. To my mind, his story fitted just a little too precisely. Almost as though he'd rehearsed it in advance.'

24

The dining room was quiet. Few tables were occupied. Archie was at a table inside a secluded alcove. He waved. As they sat on either side of him he took a package nicely wrapped out of a pocket of his tropical drill jacket, handed it to Paula.

'I have never thanked you for saving my life up on the moor. Otherwise I wouldn't be here tonight. Just a small gift.'

She opened it below the table, peeled off gold paper, removed green paper below, exposing an expensive leather case. Taking a deep breath, she unfastened the case and gasped.

Inside was a watch, its band and the watch itself studded with diamonds. Keeping it below the table she showed it to Tweed, turning to Archie.

'This is so beautiful – but it's far too much . . .'

'No more than you deserve,' Tweed commented with a smile.

'Thank you so much,' she said to Archie, 'but I can't accept it.'

'Yes, you can,' Archie responded. 'The diamonds are fake. But don't consult it in the streets of London.'

He waved to a waiter he had told to come over only when he summoned him. By this time Tweed had helped Paula fasten the present to her slim wrist and she had pushed it up her sleeve out of sight. Menus were studied, orders placed.

'I'm still stunned,' Paula said as she studied the menu.

She looked at Archie. He really was a big man with a wide chest, a large head, a neat moustache and long thick hair. In some ways he reminded her of pictures she'd seen of prophets of the Old Testament. This impression was countered by the frequent warm smile of his thick lips. He looked back.

'You'll know me next time, won't you?' He chuckled.

The three-course dinner was so good they ate almost in silence. Talk would have ruined their savouring the chef's excellent food. Then Archie signalled the waiter, who brought over a bottle he carried with extra care. Tweed stared at the label.

'Archie, that's the king of clarets. Costs a fortune!'

'Sip it first,' he advised. 'Now I'll tell you why we are here. About Black Gorse Moor . . .'

From a canvas satchel perched on the seat beyond

Paula, Archie lifted out a tightly capped plastic canister. Paula had seen him clutching it when she'd hauled him out of the hellhole. He first used large serviettes to create a concealing cloth tent. The table had already been cleared except for their glasses.

On their side of the 'tent' he placed the canister. He looked at Paula.

'Tell me what you see.'

'Four different levels of dissimilar liquids, separated by thick glass dividers.'

'An excellent start. Go on.'

'Bottom level is black as pitch, very murky. The level above is less dark with bits floating in it. Still pretty murky. How am I doing?'

'Fine so far. Now go on!' he urged.

'The liquid in the third level is lighter, but still very murky. The top level,' she concluded, 'is the purest brown-black. Almost has an oily texture—'

'Not almost,' Archie broke in. 'It is oil – of the finest quality, once treated in a refinery. Black Gorse Moor is sitting on top of endless deposits of oil. Forget Texas. I calculate there's at least enough oil there to last all Great Britain's needs for the next hundred years at least. We can forget Saudia Arabia and the rest of the OPEC blackmailers. How is the claret?'

25

After more valuable conversation with Archie, Tweed left the table and headed with Paula for the garage. Once inside he sat behind the wheel and stared ahead without moving.

'Billions and billions, Archie said the moor is worth, and Neville Guile offers Bullerton one million. He must have been furious when Archie sent him a phoney report by courier – and returned the huge fee Guile had paid him.'

'Which is why he tried to kill Archie on the moor. He spotted the fake. We'll now drive over to Hobart House. I want a word with Lord Bullerton.'

'He'll be asleep at this hour,' she protested.

'No, he won't. He told me he catnaps, then comes downstairs again and plays a game of chess against himself.'

She kept quiet until they reached the turn-off at the beginning of the Village. She leaned forward and chuckled.

'First time I've seen Mrs Grout not scrubbing her steps.'

As they approached the hole in the hedge Harry appeared, his arms waving.

'No trouble so far. Earlier there were couriers from London.'

'We know about them. Stay put. Very much on guard.'

'How else would I do that job!'

Most of the lights were still on in Hobart House. Mrs Shipton, dressed in a coat to go out, opened the door. Her hat was tilted slightly to the right. A woman in a hurry.

'What on earth do you want?' she demanded. 'At this hour!'

'To see Lord Bullerton,' Tweed replied. 'I understand he has a catnap, then comes down to play chess against himself.'

'Library.'

'Just a moment. Where on earth are you going at this hour?'

'None of your damned business.' She paused. 'This is the only time I can drive round and enjoy the fresh air. All the skivvies are out of the place long ago. Everything is ready for the morning. Anything else for your case book?'

On which note she turned to leave. But Tweed

wasn't finished with her yet. He called down the steps.

'I see there's an unmarked police car parked behind yours . . .'

'Observant, aren't we?' She clutched her Gucci handbag under one arm. 'Sergeant Marden has arrived with Lizbeth. Since his Lordship was asleep, they went straight up to her suite. Marden has excellent manners – better than some police officers I could name.'

She slipped behind the wheel of a brand-new Renault, slammed the door shut. She drove too fast up the winding road to the lane. Tweed turned to find Lance standing in the doorway. He made an off-hand gesture, looking out at the night rather than his visitors.

'The library,' he said in a superior tone.

'We know,' Tweed snapped, brushing past him.

This is getting to be familiar territory, Paula thought as Tweed knocked politely, turned the handle and descended the steps. In his smoking jacket Bullerton sat crouched over a table occupied by a chess game in progress. He frowned.

'My dear chap, welcome. And also to you, Paula. The frown was my being puzzled by the state of the game. Join me for a few moves, Tweed?'

He waited patiently while Tweed toured the board, checking it from all angles. Sitting opposite Bullerton, he moved one of his pawns. Bullerton looked perplexed.

Colin Forbes

While waiting, Tweed picked up the imposing Queen. He used a clean handkerchief to wipe off her waist a tiny mark. Then he placed her back on the board.

'She's a heavy lady,' he remarked, 'but so she should be. She dominates the entire board.'

Bullerton moved one of his pawns. Tweed immediately moved one of his. Bullerton stared.

'Checkmate!' said Tweed quietly.

'You're dangerous,' Bullerton said good-humouredly. 'I never saw that coming.'

'Archie MacBlade has told me the whole position,' Tweed explained. 'You're sitting on top of a world-class oil field. Guard it well.'

'I have already acted very quickly. I contacted my top lawyers in London. They worked incredibly fast composing an iron-clad oil trust, then two of them flew up here to the private airfield just the other side of Black Gorse Moor. I signed the document with the lawyers as witnesses. Next bit is very confidential. Trust is registered in the Bahamas where no British government can ever reach it with taxes. The registration will move tonight to another tax haven I won't name.'

'That ties it up forever.' Tweed stood up. 'I was hoping you'd moved fast. You have.'

'I gather Lizbeth has arrived under armed guard,' Paula said.

'A wonderful moment when I hugged her and she hugged me back.'

236

Paula could have sworn there were tears in his eyes. He used a coloured handkerchief and smiled. 'Your Sergeant Marden is an excellent fellow. Gets on well with Mrs Shipton, who had laid a table outside Lizbeth's door and served him a slap-up supper.'

'Must have a way with women,' Tweed said with a smile.

'One more favour, please,' he said as he approached the door. 'Who will carry on the title?'

'Since Lance refuses point-blank to be the next Lord Bullerton, I have decided Margot will be the first lady to occupy the post. In many ways she will do the job better – very brainy, superb manners and so popular, but wary of the aristos. Everyone in the house knows her, but no one outside.'

'Thank you for your time and information,' Tweed said, grasping the handle without yet turning it. 'One more thing. Are there two separate beds in Lizbeth's suite?'

'Yes, tons of room. Why?'

'Do me a favour. Let Margot sleep in Lizbeth's suite tonight and tomorrow also. Lizbeth had a bad time of it and I think she'll welcome Margot's company.'

'Chap thinks of everything,' agreed Bullerton, winking at Paula.

In the lane they were stopped briefly by Harry, who indicated he had news. Tweed lowered his window.

'Bob Newman has surfaced again,' Harry reported. 'Wants to see you urgently in the hotel garage . . .'

'More trouble,' Paula commented cheerfully as they drove out of the lane.

Entering the garage quietly, Tweed saw Marler standing by his Maserati. No sign of Newman. A well-built figure appeared, clad in a tropical-drill outfit; his wide-brimmed straw hat was pulled down over large dark glasses. For a moment Tweed didn't recognize Newman as he alighted.

'Several items you should know about,' Newman began. 'I called my pal in the East End of London. All the dangerous scum have left, including the three killers who escaped conviction in the courts on a technicality thanks to brilliant lawyers.'

Lawyers paid a fortune by Neville Guile, Paula said to herself.

'They're travelling separately,' Newman continued. 'Some in cars, some on motorbikes. Looks like the attack on you is planned for tomorrow – that is, today . . .'

'No,' said Marler. 'The day after or the one after that. They need to be fresh, to become familiar with the killing ground.'

'The other thing,' Newman went on, 'is I've discovered who Mrs Shipton really is. Don't ask me how . . .' He grinned. 'Some of my methods were unorthodox. Lived with her sister in an old small town way north of here called Barham-Downstream.

238

They ran a prosperous general store – local council had banned supermarkets. Am I going too fast?'

'No, carry on . . .'

'Her real name is Jennifer Montgomery Fisher-Mayne. Her sister was Myra Montgomery Fisher-Mayne before she married Lord Bullerton. Jennifer, who'd never met him, was furious – she'd heard about his playing about with the ladies of London. She refused to attend the wedding, made Myra promise never to admit her existence. They gossip in Barham-Downstream. So Myra never communicated with Jennifer by letter or phone. She must have wiped Jennifer out of her mind.'

'Well, well . . .' Tweed sighed. 'The one motive I overlooked was *revenge*.'

'The weather is changing dramatically,' Marler remarked. 'Three huge storms are building up north of the bridge.'

'Thanks a lot,' said Paula.

She saw the end of the glowing sun at 70°F., her favourite temperature. Her reaction showed.

Marler smiled. He waved both hands in a wide throwaway gesture.

'I don't control the weather. I hope those storms wait until we have sorted out our ambush. They break first well north of the bridge. Then the tidal wave comes.' He walked out and the others followed. He pointed across the wide stretch of grass his side of the river bank. 'Apparently once the water was less than a foot from pouring over onto the grass.'

'Wait here,' Tweed told them. 'I have a phone call to make.'

He called Hobart House. He had little hope of reaching Mrs Shipton, but felt he must try. She answered almost immediately.

'Tweed here—'

'That bulldog of yours stopped my car halfway along the lane. Quite frightening. So I drove to the end, turned round and came back to Hobart House.'

'Mrs Shipton, I really am so sorry. I would like to find a way of making it up to you . . .' Tweed, when he set out to do so, could charm the birds out of the trees. 'May I suggest we have dinner together, say tomorrow evening, at the Nag's Head? It would ease my conscience and I know I would enjoy your company, your exceptional intelligence.'

'Really?' There was a brief pause as though she had lost her breath. 'I accept your generous offer, of course. I shall indeed look forward to the occasion. I will drive over from here. Would eight o'clock be a suitable time? If not, please tell me the timing which would be convenient for you.'

'Eight would be perfect timing. I shall also warn the bulldog not to stop you. You drive a blue Renault, I believe. Then, until tomorrow evening. Goodnight to you, Mrs Shipton.'

He next called Harry and warned him not to stop a blue Renault on its way out the following evening.

And not to stop it whenever it returned. Paula ran up to him as he emerged from the garage.

'We're going to do the town. Marler's idea.'

'At this time of night!'

'The aristos have a different way of living from us. I rather like the sound of it.'

'You do?'

'And so will you. Lots of pretty women.'

Marler led the way out and Paula was astonished at the sight of the High Street, tastefully illuminated by 'Ancient Lights', the elegant Victorian lamp posts with their slanting glass panes, inside which a light glowed.

'Some of the shops are open,' she exclaimed.

'The locals, especially the aristos,' Marler explained, 'sleep late in the mornings, get up, have a light breakfast. Then they ride like mad over their great estates. In mid-afternoon they return home, have a shower, a quick snack and get some much-needed sleep. In late evening they get well dressed, come out, have a good dinner and then check out the shops. The general stores are closed – housekeepers buy the essentials during the morning.'

'Sounds like the ideal life of leisure,' Paula remarked.

'They're not idle,' Marler assured her. 'Soon they'll be hard at work, ploughing the fields, sowing the wheat. Some unusual shops. Tweed has just gone into one.'

Paula slipped into the shop: it had its name inscribed on its fascia. *Edwin Cocker*.

Tweed was gazing at a beautiful three-foot-high wooden model of a horse, painted black. The owner came forward. A tall thin man with a crooked walk, his head was long with warm eyes, his manner pleasant.

'Welcome, madame, and you, sir. I am Edwin Cocker.' He smiled again. 'I am the wood-carver of every item you see. You've seen the notice, "NO OBLIGATION WHATSOEVER TO BUY".'

'You can carve just about anything,' said Tweed, looking round at the vast array.

He wandered over to a shelf where six beautiful chess pawns stood next to each other. He picked one up, turned to Cocker.

Paula sucked in her breath as she ran her fingers over its perfect smooth surface. Tweed was paying. Cocker opened a drawer and withdrew a polished mahogany box with a snap-shut lid. Opening it she saw it was lined with pink silk. Cocker very carefully placed the pawn inside, closed the lid, presented it to Paula with a brief bow.

'I can't thank you enough,' Paula began.

'There is something else, Mr Cocker,' Tweed said. 'I hope it won't spoil this very pleasant interlude, but I need to see your register of clients.'

He began to pull out his identity folder. Cocker stopped him with a smile.

'Mr Tweed, don't look so surprised, I should think everyone in Gunners Gorge knows you by now. I am sorry but no one can see my register. Clients know that is completely confidential. I am sorry, but no one can make me break my word.'

'If you were brought before a London court the judge could – and would – insist you produced that register. I apologize for having to say that.'

'I do understand.'

'One more question, if I may. Could you, with your extraordinary skill, produce a complete set of chess pieces?'

'Yes . . .' Cocker paused. 'It would take time.'

'It really has been a unique pleasure knowing you.' Tweed held out his hand and Cocker grasped it. Tweed lowered his voice. 'There will be no order for you to appear before any judge.'

'I was shocked by your threatening him with a court order,' Paula commented.

'On a murder investigation I use any method to get information.'

Marler met them outside. He seemed in an exceptionally good mood.

'Better get back to the hotel. Everyone, including Harry, has to be in the dining room for breakfast by 3.30 a.m. The landlord was very cooperative.'

'3.30 a.m!' echoed Paula. 'What on earth for?'

'I told you, breakfast. Then we drive along the High Street so you can see the battlefield. Harry has kindly let me drive his inconspicuous grey Fiat . . .'

Entering the deserted lobby, the buoyant Marler slapped Paula very gently on her rump.

'Sleep well,' he said. 'It will be a quiet day.'

'When someone predicts that,' she snapped back, 'the day turns out to be anything but quiet.'

26

The pallid grey dawn transformed Gunners Gorge as they drove slowly out of the garage. Marler was behind the wheel with Tweed alongside him. Paula shared the back with Harry.

'I don't know how you managed it,' Paula said.

'Managed what?' Harry growled.

'Breakfast. You had a three-egg omelette, crispy bacon and fried potatoes.' She chuckled. 'You'll put on weight.'

'No, he won't,' Tweed called back. 'Had his annual check at the beginning of the year. The doctor said he'd never seen a fitter man.'

Paula was peering out. The town looked weird as the dawn light spread over it: more like a frightening ghost town. The streets had recently been hosed down by night workers. Not a soul to be seen.

Colin Forbes

Halfway along the High Street, Marler dipped his
head to gaze up through the windscreen. When they
reached a layby he swung into it, stopped, turned off
the engine.

'Someone is watching from the top of the ridge. Be
back in a minute. Everyone stay in the car . . .'

Diving out, he began climbing rapidly up a steep
gulley. He paused frequently to listen. Nothing. He
continued climbing, avoiding beds of pebbles, which
would make a noise, and made his way up to the
summit over a grassy area. At the top he peered over.
A short distance to his left stood a heavily built man
peering through a large telescope mounted on a
tripod. The telescope was aimed at the caves on the
far side of the Falls.

Marler remained quite still as the man turned his
head, then went back to staring through the telescope.
Marler knew now who and what he was. Dangerous.
Very slowly he eased his way across the grass on the
summit. Then he hauled the Smith & Wesson revolver
he had borrowed from Bob Newman out of his shoulder holster, tucked it down inside his belt.

He suddenly leapt up, ran, his long legs covering the
ground swiftly. His target heard him coming, bent
down to an open satchel on the ground, came up
holding a stiletto-like knife. He swung round. By then
Marler was behind him. The heavy barrel of the
revolver crashed down on his head. As the target
sagged, the barrel descended again with all Marler's
force.

Checking the man as he lay crumpled on the ground, Marler found no sign of a pulse. A few yards beyond the telescope on its tripod was a steep, narrow gulch. Pebbles covered its entrance, then came smooth rock, ending abruptly where more rocks had blocked any exit.

Marler lifted the body, hands under its armpits, dragged it to the top of the gulch, shoved it down. The corpse slid rapidly down over the pebbles like a toboggan. It continued its journey until it hit the blocked exit and lay still.

Marler threw the dropped knife into the gulch and, after a quick look, the satchel with neatly arranged pockets for different knives.

Next he gazed through the telescope, which had a nightsight. He found he was staring into the shallow cave at level one on the other side of the Falls.

'Thought so,' he said to himself.

Heaving up the whole apparatus, he flung it into the gulch. In doing so, one of the tripod legs caught briefly in a drystone wall perched on the opposite edge. Several large stones broke loose and fell into the gulch. Which gave him another idea.

He walked round the top of the gulch, sat down on the far side, placed his boots against the wall. He took a deep breath, heaved against it with all his strength.

The whole wall collapsed into the gulch. It nearly took him with it. Marler grabbed a gorse bush, which saved him. Easing himself back from the drop, he stood up, walked back round the end, peered down. The dawn light was stronger.

All he could see was a jumbled pile of rocks. No sign of the body, no sign of the telescope, no sign of anything. He clapped both hands lightly, then scampered back down the route he had ascended, slipped behind the wheel.

'What happened?' Tweed asked.

'I'd underestimated Lepard's caution. He placed a chap with a large telescope up there, aimed at the caves. Purpose – to make sure we hadn't discovered them and had people checking them out. A nasty piece of work monitoring the telescope. Chap called Pearl Kerwald.'

'Pearl is a girl's name,' Paula said.

'A nickname. His technique was to patrol Bond Street, Mayfair, areas like that. He'd see a well-dressed woman with a string of pearls round her neck, grab her from behind, use a sharp knife to cut the rope near the clasp. There were cases when his knife slipped and he'd cut her throat. He'd throw her over the bonnet of a parked car, yell, "Heart attack!" and disappear.'

'Where is he now?' Paula pressed.

'Somewhere inside that small mountain. They said twelve thugs coming up. One down, eleven to go . . .'

'You've tactfully left out the one I had to strangle,' she told him, squeezing his shoulder.

'OK,' he agreed as he pulled out into the street and

headed north. 'If you insist, two down and ten to go . . .'

Paula could now hear the muted rumble and roar as thousands of gallons of water poured down over the Falls. A good mile further north they passed the old iron road bridge linking Ascot Row with the High Street.

Paula was staring to her right at the scenic beauty. Vast fields of grass spread out as far as the eye could see. The endless green she found soothing with the silence of the open country. Ahead was a huge six-exit roundabout.

Signposts indicated routes to towns Tweed knew were a long way north. The fifth exit, as Marler circled the roundabout, pointed to London.

'That's their escape route,' he remarked. 'Ours too if it all goes wrong.'

'Be confident,' Paula said sharply.

'A good planner,' Tweed explained to her, 'always has his escape route worked out.'

They drove slowly back towards the hotel through still deserted streets. The air remained very crisp. As they approached a sign with the word Marcantonio's, Archie MacBlade ran down the steps, waved for them to stop.

'I've booked a table upstairs at the Gold Bowl for all of you. Breakfast awaits . . .'

'We had it earlier,' Paula protested.

'Sure you're not hungry again?' Archie said with a warm smile.

Paula suddenly realized she was ravenous. It must be the air, which had a nip of cold in it. Archie guided Marler up a narrow street to a car park at the back. They returned to the front. He led them up a flight of steps and inside.

'I could eat a horse,' said Harry.

'Not on the menu,' Archie chaffed him. 'You'll wish there was somewhere like this in London. Locals come, eat breakfast and then go back home and sleep ready for the day's riding. They were here finishing breakfast when you drove past earlier. Come on . . .'

They entered a tastefully furnished hall and, led by Archie, stepped inside a spacious elevator. The panel had three buttons. Archie produced a black card, inserted it into a slot, then pressed the top button.

'Can't get to the Golden Bowl without inserting the card,' he explained.

A small man in evening clothes with a long thin moustache was waiting for them. He bowed.

'Welcome, Mr MacBlade – and your friends.'

He showed them into a large circular restaurant. Paula looked up. The ceiling was a golden bowl. Archie spoke as they sat at a large circular table.

'This is Marco, the owner. The beautiful woman with him is his sister, Benita.'

'I supervise the kitchen,' she said, looking with a warm smile at Paula. 'Your orders, please. Anything.'

'Could I have two fried eggs, crispy bacon and fried potatoes?'

'Of course, ma'mselle.'

Harry ordered three fried eggs with all the trimmings, and so it went on. Marco returned with a silver bucket, tripod and a bottle of expensive champagne. Paula stared.

'It is a champagne breakfast,' Archie said. 'The feast is on me.'

Marco used a towel to wipe the bottle dry, removed the metal covering then the cork, sniffed it. Tweed was leaning forward, gazing.

'What's fascinating you?' Paula asked.

'His skill.'

Service of the first-class food was swift. Paula plunged her knife and fork into a fried egg, cleaned her plate at the same moment as the others. She had sipped her champagne and then drunk the whole glass.

Greetings were exchanged with Marco and his sister. Paula was leaving when Benita gently tucked a black card inside the top pocket of her leather jacket.

'Welcome at any time,' she whispered in her soft voice.

Archie remained and they returned to the car. As they were leaving, Paula and Tweed were now in the back, and she nudged him.

'I'm going back to sleep.'

'So am I,' he said. He paused. 'That is the most important breakfast I've ever had,' he stated.

'Important?'

'Important.'

27

Paula couldn't get to sleep. She changed position, tossed and turned. No good. She shouldn't have drunk that whole glass of champagne. She gave up trying to sleep.

Jumping out of bed, she dressed again. Checking the time, she went quietly into the garage. 9.45 a.m. Marler waved to her. She joined him.

Tweed was behind the wheel of the Audi, about to depart. He lowered the window, called out to her.

'Couldn't sleep? Go back, have another shower.'

The Audi crawled out of the garage, proceeded slowly up the High Street. Paula clenched her fists inside the pockets of her tunic. Marler, sensing her tension, put an arm round her waist.

In the far distance, way north of the bridge, she saw a brief brilliant lightning flash. Everywhere the sky was a molten menacing grey.

'I do wish I was with him,' she said. 'Could it be today?'

'Definitely not. The thugs have not taken up position in those caves. I'm just hoping that triple storm holds off until we've done the job. Forecast says it will arrive in the late morning. As to Tweed, he has to keep up what they think is his daily routine.'

From the Audi, Tweed was observing housekeepers entering the general store and other shops. The air had turned heavy, sultry. A prelude to the expected rage of the gathering storm.

Behind his net curtain, Lepard watched as Tweed passed his window at twenty-five miles an hour. He squeezed his clawlike hands together, his face twisted in a sadistic smile.

'Enjoy your last day on earth, Mr Tweed,' he said aloud.

When Tweed returned to the garage he found Paula still standing by Marler's side. He frowned as he alighted.

'Paula, I told you to get back to bed.'

'I'm going now. Wanted to see you safely back.'

'Well, now you've seen me, kindly shove off.'

'You look heavy-eyed,' she told him. 'Plenty of sleep for you too. You have that dinner here with Mrs Shipton this evening. She's sharp.'

'Sharp as a knife. And she's rapidly moving up my shortlist of suspects . . .'

In his suite, Tweed forced himself to take a quick

shower. He phoned Dowling, asked for a wake-up call at 6 p.m. Putting on his pyjamas he got into bed. The moment his head rested on the pillow he fell into a deep sleep.

He swore to himself in the evening when the phone rang, picked it up, thanked Dowling. His wristwatch showed precisely 6 p.m. He felt amazingly fresh.

Putting on his best suit, he went downstairs into the dining room, booked a table in a secluded alcove with its back to the wall. Returning to his room he found a note inside an envelope pushed under his door.

To give you the privacy you need I'm dining elsewhere with Newman and Archie. Love, Paula.

She thinks of everything, he said to himself. Taking some care, he brushed his hair, put on his jacket again. Always in earlier interviews he had worn his working suit. He knew a smart appearance impressed women.

He was in the hall when Mrs Shipton drove up in her Renault. A servant rushed forward to park it.

'Now, you listen to me,' she began in her imperious manner. 'There are several other cars in the garage. Therefore you will be most careful not to scratch the body of my car. I shall examine it scrupulously when I have had dinner!'

She remained a distance from him, extending her hand, compelling him to walk to her. In her most queenly mood, Tweed was thinking.

He showed her to the table. She looked archly at him as she slid along the banquette into the corner.

'Now you've got me penned in if you say something I don't like.'

'It's easier for me to order dinner from this seat,' he replied casually.

They had placed their orders when they both stared. A new diner had walked in by himself. Falkirk. He chose a table just far away to be unable to hear what they said, then summoned a waiter. Between them they shifted the angle of the table, and Falkirk sat down.

'You see what the swine has done?' Mrs Shipton said viciously.

'He's angled the table so he's not observing us directly. But he only has to switch his gaze a fraction to check on us. I notice you don't like him much.'

'He's a private detective . . .'

'I know.' Tweed sipped the Chablis he'd ordered, nodded.

'He's also a blackmailer. I should know. He blackmailed me.'

Tweed was taken aback. Nothing showed in his expression as he forked his soufflé into his mouth. He was also watching the man who was standing well back in the entrance to the dining room, surveying every diner. In his hand he was holding a mobile phone.

It was Lance. Very smartly dressed, as always, he

wore an electric-blue two-piece suit and a pink shirt. One moment he was there. The next moment he vanished.

'That was Lance,' Mrs Shipton said. 'Looking for a female victim for the evening.'

'Possibly,' said Tweed.

'Nothing here to suit his exotic taste.'

'How did Falkirk try to blackmail you?' Tweed asked suddenly.

'I let that slip.'

'And now,' Tweed said firmly, 'you have to tell me the whole story. I don't have to remind you—'

'That you are investigating a triple murder,' she said, mimicking him.

'Stop pussyfooting. I need to know.'

'I hired Falkirk when he came to Hobart House looking for business . . .'

'Hired him to do what?' demanded Tweed.

'To check out whether Myra had been murdered, all those years ago.'

'*Why?*' Tweed pressed harder, his voice tougher.

'Well, if it had been Lord Bullerton maybe I was in a dangerous position. I'm often alone with him in the house.'

'You mentioned blackmail by Falkirk. Tell me.'

'I hired him . . .' She hesitated. 'To look for evidence that Myra had been murdered. Pushed over the Falls.'

'You've started. Might as well tell me the lot.'

'He said his fee would be roughly five hundred pounds. Then he came back and said he couldn't ___ any evidence. He said his fee would be five *thousand* pounds. Then he whispered he didn't think Lord Bullerton would like what I had done at all.' Her voice trembled with fury. 'I paid. Lord Bullerton and I were getting on rather well,' she added coyly.

'If this factor has a vital bearing on the case—'

He stopped speaking as something extraordinary happened. Sable, clad in riding kit, had stormed into the dining room, was heading for their table fast. She stood before them, hands on hips, shouting at the top of her voice.

'So she's got you, the master detective, hooked too! Did you know she's got every man hooked between her legs? She is nothing but an evil tart . . .' A string of obscenities was shrieked, her face distorted in a malicious sneer. 'Been to bed with her yet? Or is this dinner the flaming prelude?'

The whole restaurant was staring. Tweed was reluctant to get up, fearing a physical tussle with her. Two men came in, Harry and Marler. Harry was carrying a towel soaked in water.

They came swiftly up behind her. Marler grabbed her arms, Harry used his wet towel to wrap round her mouth, making sure she could breathe. They frog-marched her to the exit. Marler smiled at his audience as he drawled quickly at them, 'She gets like this every six months. She's seeing a doctor . . .' Then the three disappeared through the exit. Diners started eating again. Some had their heads together speculating on the dramatic scene they had witnessed.

'I think we'd better leave,' whispered Mrs Shipton.

'The last move to make. And I'm enjoying this super soufflé. Don't you like the look of yours?'

'I suppose you're right.'

'I often am, Ms Montgomery Fisher-Mayne. Do you ever miss the atmosphere of Barham-Downstream?'

'What!' she screeched quietly. 'What the hell did you say?'

Tweed had chosen the right psychological moment. 'Mrs Shipton' was off balance, still reeling from Sable's embarrassing attack.

'I was being polite, addressing you by your real name. I also mentioned where you had come from. Why, after such a long time, did you come here – *such* a long time after Myra's murder?'

'What! She *was* murdered, then?'

'I doubt I'll ever prove it. Too long ago.'

'You're confusing me . . .'

'That was one of the best soufflés I've ever tasted. Ms Fisher-Mayne, did *you* kill her? For leaving you to struggle with the general store alone? Hatred sometimes takes years to build up.'

'You're so insulting. No, I did not murder her. I came to see what sort of a life she had led. That horrible Sable has upset me. She drinks brandy. She was a walking barrel of it tonight. I saw the tables she passed smell it.'

'She was, of course, summoned here. Someone

phoned Hobart House. Two candidates for the crime, Falkirk and Lance. Unless you told her yourself to break up our interview.'

'You have the most devious mind . . .'

'I admit it.' Tweed called for the bill. Then he accompanied her safely to her Renault.

She said not a word. Slamming the door, she revved up the engine, drove out too fast without a glance in his direction. When he re-entered the hall, Newman had just returned with Paula from dinner. They were talking to Marler, who spoke to Tweed.

'Harry has returned to his watching post near Hobart House. I called him when I saw Sable staggering out of her car. I've a nose for trouble.'

'Thank you both,' Tweed said. 'It was beginning to look like a dog fight.'

'D-Day tomorrow,' Marler said cheerfully. 'Lepard has his thugs in position inside the caves on the other side of the Falls.'

'I see nothing to be cheerful about,' Paula commented.

28

When Tweed climbed the stairs to get some sleep, Paula came up close behind him. She waited while he unlocked and opened his door.

'May I have a few words with you?' she asked.

'Of course.'

He thought she wanted a brief résumé of his encounter with Mrs Shipton. Or she wanted to pass on information obtained during her dinner. She closed the door, stood with her arms folded.

'I'm coming with you in the Audi.'

'No! You are not.'

'We *always* do things together,' she insisted.

'Not this time. They expect to see only one person in the car with me.'

'So I'll huddle down out of sight in the back.'

'No, you won't, because you won't be there.'

'Snapping at me will get you nowhere,' she retorted.

'I'm telling you, Paula, it's not on.'

'And I'm telling you it is on, so accept it.'

'I could give you a direct order.'

'Give it, then, if it'll make you feel better.'

'As Deputy Chief of the SIS I am giving you a direct order. You will obey it.'

'All right. Better get to bed. You won't get much sleep.'

Her stubborn mood seemed to have vanished. She kissed him on the cheek, went along to her room.

Once inside she phoned room service, ordered a large breakfast to be served in her room at 4 a.m, then requested a wake-up call for 3.30 a.m.

Before a quick shower she took from the wardrobe a dark jacket and trousers. She had never before worn them. They were so sombre they merged with the dark.

29

The following morning at nine thirty the air was intolerably humid. The sky was a solid grey. Just north of the bridge beyond the Falls a vast storm moved slowly south.

In the garage, Marler was having a last word with Tweed, who sat behind the wheel of the Audi. As they talked a shadow moved in the darkness.

'They're in position in the caves,' Marler drawled. 'Lepard is with them as leader. So are we – in position on this side. With a bit of luck we'll have wiped them out before that king of a storm breaks. It's a monster. I'd better get into my position.'

Tweed started the engine, began to crawl out of the garage. A rear door was opened, shut. In his rear-view mirror Tweed saw Paula crouching down in the back.

He swore inwardly. There was nothing he could do. He had to keep moving to meet the delicate timetable. He said not one word. Neither did Paula.

She was checking the Browning she'd extracted from her shoulder holster. At the training mansion hidden in deepest Surrey they had been taught to do this in darkness.

As they proceeded along the High Street they passed noticeboards Marler had had erected in the middle of the night.

KEEP OFF STREETS, PAVEMENTS THIS MORNING. ABOUT TO BE TARRED. OK TO WALK ON AFTER 3 PM TODAY.

It was the only way to protect the inhabitants of the town when the bullets began to fly.

There was a sinister rumble of thunder. No rain drenching down yet. Paula opened the roadside window, looking out on the steep-stepped roads mounting the hill overlooking the High Street. No more thunder. It was ominously quiet.

On the far side of the Falls, Lepard was struggling with a special weapon. The bazooka was like a drain-pipe. The sticky atmosphere was making his hands moist. It was not easy to manoeuvre the heavy unfamiliar weapon.

In front of him, lying down below the low rampart

wall at the rim of the cave, three of his elite men perched the barrels of their rifles, aimed at the oncoming Audi. They found themselves exposed with shoulders and heads above the parapet. It was the only way they could see down at the oncoming target, the Audi crawling closer by the minute.

Below them at Level Two their compatriots faced the same problem. They were nervous about their exposure. It was a difficulty Lepard had not foreseen.

The men below them in the cave at Level Three were equally nervous. Lepard had told everyone the signal to open fire would be when he fired the rocket from his own weapon, the deadly bazooka. One hit from his weapon and Tweed would be eliminated in a burst of fire.

Marler, perched high up on the roof of a house, had also spotted the weapon, through the cross-hairs of his Armalite. Beside him Harry had his automatic aimed at the cave in Level Two.

'What do you think?' Harry asked.

'It's going to be tricky. At Level One, Lepard has a bazooka.'

'Lord help us . . .'

'One rocket hitting the target and it's all over. I'm happy to see Lepard is unfamiliar with the weapon. It keeps wobbling all over the place. When I open fire so do the rest of our people.'

'Well, Pete Nield has arrived from the training mansion in Surrey, and he and Newman are covering that lot at Level Three . . .'

Lepard inserted his deadly rocket. It coincided with the storm breaking over the Falls with a tremendous thunderclap. An incredible cascade poured down from the sky, millions of gallons flooded down over the Falls.

Marler fired his first shot. The bullet took half Lepard's face away. Blood poured down. Marler's first bullet had hit as Lepard was about to press the trigger. He lost control. The barrel was aimed up at the roof of the rocky cave, brought it down.

Lepard was sliced in half at the waist as a huge knife-like rock caught him. Marler's bombardment was nonstop as his men sprayed the caves. The top half of Lepard's body, streaming with blood, fell into the surge of water, which was now a small Niagara. The rest of his body went over the edge, followed by his compatriots blasted by the shock-wave.

Inside the Audi, Paula stared in amazement. The immense surge of water was no longer white. It was blood-red as other enemies toppled out of the caves at Levels Two and Three. The Falls had taken on the look of a huge rainbow.

Paula stared down at the large pool at the base of the Falls. Enemy bodies floated on its crimson surface, rushed on downriver as they were caught up in the swift surge of the central current, much enlarged. She averted her gaze.

The action was taking on the atmosphere of a pounding operatic drama – but one never seen in the theatre. Vast sheets of rain hammered the roof of the Audi. A deafening inferno swept Gunners Gorge. The foetid atmosphere was creating a mist creeping up over the Falls.

Marler, now clad in a green sou'wester, was searching the area. He was perched on a flat rock to evade the streams of water sluicing down the ridge.

'Harry,' he shouted, 'something's wrong. There were ten of them. I counted. No sign of the tenth man. Where is he?'

Inside the Audi, where Tweed was slowly turning the vehicle to face the Nag's Head, Paula caught motion out of the corner of her eye. The tenth man was clambering fast down a water-logged gulley. His target was the Audi.

In his right hand he held a grenade. Paula tensed. If he got closer he only had to remove the pin and roll it under the Audi's petrol tank. One flash, one explosion and they'd be roasted, liquidated.

She threw open the rear door, jumped out. Rain drenched her. Gripping her Browning in both hands, she fired twice. Distorted red flower shapes appeared on the tunic covering his chest. He fell forward onto the grenade.

She froze, waiting for the detonation. Nothing happened. Later, when explosives expert Harry carefully lifted the body, he found the pin had not been withdrawn from the grenade.

Paula was about to jump back into the Audi when she glanced across at the river bank. Lord Bullerton, stomping through sheets of rain, stopped by his stone asking for Lizbeth's return. To destroy it now she was safely home?

No one had thought of telling him to remain at Hobart House. He stepped forward a few more paces. The rain had churned the river bank into a muddy swamp. He slipped, fell into the river, hands grabbing at sturdy shrubs.

Appalled, she ran across the marshy ground. He was struggling to get out, up to his broad chest in water, getting nowhere. She leant down, inserted a hand under each of his armpits. He was too heavy for her to haul him out.

Movement caught her attention nearer the Falls. She stared. Neville Guile's long legs were carrying him towards the bank on her side. Stripping off his white jacket and slip-on shoes, he dived into the river. She understood. He had felt compelled to see with his own eyes the killing of Tweed.

There was a brief near-comic element when she saw he was heading for the opposite bank. A Rolls-Royce

waited for him. By the side of the road opposite a uniformed chauffeur stood to attention.

Guile was a surprisingly strong swimmer, cleverly
swimming at an angle into the main force of the current.

'Oh, my God!' she said aloud.

A massive tree trunk, caught up by a fresh storm
which had burst recently well north of the bridge, creating a tidal surge of water, dropped the hundred and
fifty feet into the pool below. It was swept out and carried downriver.

'Oh, no!' Paula called out in her terror.

The 'tree' was a full-grown crocodile, far from its
normal hunting ground. The prehistoric monster
headed towards Guile. Only the head was visible now,
exposing its evil little eyes.

Guile only saw it coming when he was more than
halfway across the river. He panicked, began to dog-
paddle. The beast's enormous jaws were now fully
open. It reached the swimming man. His whole body
was sucked inside. It had stopped raining and was
ominously quiet. She clearly heard the crunch of
Guile's skull as the creature closed its jaws. She looked
away.

Now she was confronted with a new terror. Blood
from Bullerton's damaged knee was flowing into the
current. Crocodiles have a deadly scent for the presence of blood. The creature, having had its main
course, was now ready for dessert as it headed inshore
for Bullerton. Paula was in despair. She knew that

bullets would simply bounce off its thick wrinkled hide, but she knew she couldn't heave out Bullerton's heavy body.

She heard swift feet running and slithering in the mud. Harry was tearing across towards her at astonishing speed. At school he had excelled as a cricketer, a brilliant bowler. In his right hand he held the largest grenade Paula had ever seen.

The beast was no more than fifty feet from the helpless Bullerton. Standing close to her, Harry watched as the awful jaws opened. He took a firm stand, removed the pin, lobbed the grenade. It landed deep inside the open jaws, was caught in the crocodile's throat.

The detonation was muffled. Paula stared as the monster was fragmented, small pieces flying across the river into the main current. They looked like pieces of bark from a big tree.

'I'll take over,' Harry told her.

Bending down carefully, he exchanged hands with Paula, inserting them under Bullerton's armpits. One mighty heave and Bullerton was lying on firm ground. He stood up, seeming to be none the worse for his ordeal.

A gentle hand descended on Paula's shoulder. An equally gentle voice spoke. Tweed's.

'A snack lunch I think, Paula, then plenty of sleep. We have to go out this evening to confront the murderer of four people.'

'Four!' she exclaimed.

'Yes. *Four.*'

30

It was an overcast, moonless night when Tweed, with Paula, drove his Audi down the slope to Hobart House beyond the hedge-lined lane. It was incredibly silent, which unsettled Paula.

Few lights glowed. A dim light illuminated the windows of the library. As Tweed parked, Paula thought she saw two vague shadows crossing the bowl. She looked again and there was nothing. Imagination.

Her uncertain observation vanished as the glare lights flooded the terrace and steps. She wondered who would open the door. It was a grim-looking Mrs Shipton, still fully dressed.

'At this hour?' she hissed venomously.

'Kindly let us in,' Tweed said calmly.

'If you've come to see me it's a waste of time. I've just taken a sedative. After all those horrors in Gunners Gorge . . .'

'So you were there, you witnessed what happened?'

'I've got to get to bed. I have to climb those stairs before the sedative starts working.'

She stood aside, closed the door after them, pointed a finger at the library and began to haul herself up the stairs. They waited to make sure she made it, unless she had lied.

Halfway up the stairs she turned, her arm extended as her long index finger pointed again at the library.

Paula took a firmer grip on the long evidence envelope with the ancient green mop handle inside. Tweed had asked her to be sure to bring it.

Opening the door of the dim-lit library, Tweed walked down the steps, followed by Paula. Seated in an imposing antique chair behind a heavy wooden table was Lance, wearing a smart dark suit. On the table was spread out the chessboard with a game in progress. His face was very white in the poor lighting.

'Good evening, both of you,' he said with a pleasant smile. 'Please join me.'

He gestured towards a large couch pushed close to the side of the table facing him. Paula had difficulty squeezing in the narrow space between table and couch. Tweed experienced the same problem. He looked at Lance as Paula placed the old mop handle at the edge beyond the chessboard. Lance didn't even glance at it. Tweed's voice was grim when he spoke.

'Lance Mandeville, I have come to arrest you for quadruple murder. Anything you say—'

'Oh, I know the old rigmarole,' Lance said amiably. 'But quadruple is four.'

'You started on your career of murder early. You pushed Lady Bullerton into the Falls. Concealed behind Aaron's Rock, you shoved the working end of that mop into her back.'

'Fascinating. I didn't think this was a social call.' He slipped his hand inside his jacket, produced a silver cigarette case. 'Smoke?'

When they both shook their heads he returned the case to his jacket. Tweed continued to speak in his grim tone.

'Your next excursion into murder was locating your missing sisters. You checked their night-time movements, waited, cut their throats and mutilated their faces so no newspaper pictures would appear appealing for identification. Your method was horrible.' Tweed picked up the chess Queen, used both hands to unscrew it round the waist, revealing a long corkscrew. 'Undoubtedly it was made by that brilliant woodworker in the High Street. You probably told him some story about wanting to surprise a party – by unscrewing the Queen and using the corkscrew to open a bottle of wine.'

'Sounds an interesting chap.' Lance smirked. 'Where is his shop?'

'You know. You visited him. He keeps a register of clients. In the High Court the judge can compel him to open the register. That alone will be damning evidence.'

'You clever old thing.' Lance smirked again.

'You killed the two oldest sisters in London because your father teased you about a daughter inheriting the title. You took him seriously so the sisters had to go.'

'Really? They'd have been lousy at the job.'

Paula sat appalled, speechless at the incredible callousness he was displaying.

'You knew about the huge oil field. You are the informant who kept Neville Guile in touch with my activities.'

'He paid well for my information, you know.' Lance's manner towards Tweed became condescending.

'Then your final murder victim was Hartland Trent. No point in letting him get a slice of such a gigantic pie. What put me on to you were two things. In this house you struck an attitude that you'd no interest at all in eventually becoming the next Lord Bullerton. Yet in the town, among your host of girl friends, you assured them you *would* inherit the title. You made a bad mistake a few minutes ago. You referred to the woodworker's *shop*. I never mentioned that he had one. We have enough evidence to send you down for three life sentences with no option ever for parole.'

'You really are a clever old thing.' He gave a ghastly smile.

Lance had been drinking when they arrived. From the odour drifting across the table Paula thought it was gin. The strange glass he had been using was more like a tankard with a very thick base. He now used it to emphasize what he was saying, hammering it on the table.

'I am a good organizer.' He slid his hand inside his jacket and they expected the silver cigarette case to appear again. Instead, his hand reappeared holding a Walther, which he aimed point-blank at Paula.

'I . . . am . . . a . . . good . . . organizer,' he began, hammering down the glass.

Paula heard the faint sound of tinkling glass. She looked at the base of the tankard. It was intact.

'Everything is prepared,' he continued, no longer punctuating his words with the glass. 'I expected you to come. I have left a long wide gardener's barrow at the end of the terrace. I'll lay your bodies alongside each other. I have the strength to push its well-oiled wheels up to Black Gorse Moor. There the bodies will be tipped into one of the deep tunnels, then covered with rocks and pebbles.

'Don't make a move, Mr Tweed,' he warned. 'Otherwise the first bullet will ruin Miss Grey's head. Then I shall have ample time to shoot you . . .'

The explosive bullet removed his whole jaw. Synchronized, two rifle bullets hit him in the chest. Tweed never forgot the macabre scene. In slumping down across the chessboard, Lance's right hand fell on the bisected waist of the Queen.

Paula jerked her head towards the closed red velvet curtains. Window panes smashed. Harry reached in to turn the handle, rifle tucked under his arm, entering the library followed by Marler gripping the Armalite which had fired the explosive bullet.

'I thought it best to take precautions,' Tweed remarked.

'You might have told me,' she protested.

'Then you might not have acted naturally.'

Police sirens howled in the distance. Coming closer to the town from the south.

'That's reinforcements to wipe all the blood from the caves,' Marler said. 'An advance unit arrived earlier. Buchanan is coming himself.'

'I can see him in London,' Tweed said, taking Paula by the arm. 'We'll have a quick snack dinner at the hotel. Set your alarm clock for 6 a.m. I want to be back before dusk.'

Epilogue

The following evening they were about to turn into Park Crescent. It was a brilliant sunny end to a day when the weather had been perfect all the way south. Paula was gazing at everything.

'You know,' she said to Tweed, 'it's a wonderful experience to *visit* the countryside. All those vast areas of greenery and forests. I would one day like to go back but I'm so glad to get home.'

'I agree,' responded Tweed. 'It's familiar surroundings so you feel at home here. Despite the rush and the bustle. All the variety of a great city.'

He turned into Park Crescent, stopped the Audi close to the kerb below the entrance to their headquarters. She was looking at him.

'What is it?' he asked.

'You are about to court-martial me for direct disobedience, for jumping into the back of this car just before all the fireworks up at Gunners Gorge. Am I right?'

'Yes, you are. I'm about to pronounce sentence.'

'Which is?' she enquired, nervously plucking at her skirt.

'A long leisurely evening, with dinner at the Ritz.'

Simon & Schuster and Pocket Books
are proud to present

THE MAIN CHANCE

Colin Forbes

Available in paperback
ISBN 978-1-4165-1123-6

Turn the page to read an extract from
The Main Chance . . .

Prologue

There was nothing to warn Tweed he was setting out on the strangest case of his career, as Deputy Director of the SIS and, earlier, as Scotland Yard's ace detective.

It was a glorious March day as he drove well south of London with his second-in-command, Paula Grey, seated beside him. She studied a map, navigating for him; they had left the motorway on her instructions, were now driving south-west along a wide country road. On either side rose steep banks topped with hedges, green leaf-shoots already showing. The sun shone down out of a clear blue sky. Occasionally they passed an isolated house, its front garden covered with crocuses and sheaves of daffodils.

'This is the life,' Paula remarked, glancing out of the window. Attractive, slim, thirty-something, jet black hair reaching her neck framed a well-shaped face.

'Any idea where we're going?' Tweed asked.

'Of course I have. Hengistbury Manor is buried

deep inside what they call The Forest, which is vast. A weird area to site the headquarters of the Main Chance Bank.'

'Richest private bank in the world, so Buchanan said.'

It had started early that morning, when Tweed arrived at SIS headquarters, at Park Crescent in London. All his key staff were assembled in his spacious first-floor office. The tall ex-reporter Bob Newman sprawled in an armchair. Typically, Harry Butler, the Cockney, perched on the floor, Paula sat at her desk in a corner near the windows. Marler, ace marksman, stood next to Pete Nield.

Tweed had hardly settled behind his antique desk, a present from his staff, when the phone rang. He raised his eyebrows. 8 a.m. Who was calling at this hour?

Monica, his secretary for many years, a middle-aged woman who wore her hair tied back in a bun, answered. Covering the mouthpiece she called out: 'Commander Buchanan of the Yard is phoning you urgently.'

'Bit early, Roy,' Tweed began, after signalling Paula to listen in on her extension.

'It's an emergency,' Buchanan's crisp voice told him. 'I need to ask you an important favour. You've heard of the Main Chance Bank, richest in this country, maybe in the world. Totally independent. No shares on the

Stock Exchange. Controlled by Bella Main. Eighty-four years old with all her marbles. Met you at a party a year ago. Was very impressed. Could you make it down to see her today?'

'Where is she?'

'Hengistbury Manor. Located in an area called The Forest.'

'So where the devil is that?'

Paula, a map open, was signalling. She had already located it. Tweed nodded, spoke again to Buchanan.

'Forget that question. Paula has it. Now why on earth does Bella Main want to see me?'

'I don't know. She wouldn't say . . .'

'Roy,' Tweed growled, 'then why is it important to you, for Heaven's sake?'

'The government thinks there's something funny about that bank.'

'Funny in what way?' Tweed demanded.

'I don't know.' Buchanan was sounding desperate. 'I think maybe several rich ministers have money in the bank. Just a guess. But at the moment I'm choked up with my present job, all my present problems. You know I've been appointed Commander of the Anti-Terrorist Squad? Please make the effort. Could be important . . .'

'In what way?'

'No idea.'

'You're a barrel of information. When does she expect me?'

'This morning, Tweed. As near eleven as you can make it. I've made an appointment on your behalf.'

'Without consulting me? Thanks a lot!'

'I'm sorry, but I'm really in a jam. I told her you might take Paula with you. I do apologize.'

'Get back to chasing terrorists. We'll go. You owe me a big one.' Tweed slammed down the phone before Buchanan could say anything else, looked across at Paula. 'Is it easy to find?'

'No, but I'll get us there.' She turned to Harry, who was peering over her shoulder. 'Why are you so interested?'

'Just curious about where you're going.' He jabbed a thick finger on her map. 'That's it?'

'Yes, it is.' She stood up. 'I'd better put something on. It could be chilly down there. And Tweed is pawing the floor.' Her chief had already slipped on a camel-hair overcoat, was standing by the door. She was inside a fur-lined leather jacket in seconds. She sat on her chair, checked her 6.35mm Beretta automatic was tucked snugly inside the holster attached to her lower right leg. She had earlier checked the 7.65mm was inside her hip holster. She jumped up.

'Ready and willing!'

'Then let's get moving,' Tweed said.

The phone rang. Tweed shook his head as Monica answered. 'I'm not here,' he warned.

'You are for this one,' Monica told him. 'It's Philip

Cardon. From abroad as usual, I expect.'

Tweed perched on the edge of his desk, signalled to Paula, who darted back to her desk. They lifted their receivers at the same moment. Tweed's impatience was replaced by a tone of genuine pleasure.

'Philip, you old dog. Haven't heard from you for ages. How is the world?'

'Is this line secure?' Philip's voice was unusually abrupt.

'If it isn't we're out of business.'

'This call will be brief. I have a deep-cover agent. He tells me Calouste Doubenkian is on his way to Britain. Could be there already. You know who I mean?'

'Vaguely. Never made his acquaintance.'

'You don't want to. He's very dangerous, enormously powerful. My information is that he's on his way in connection with something concerning you.'

'In what respect, Philip? I can't imagine why.'

'Neither can I. But watch your back. I'll call when I've dug up more data.'

Tweed heard a click. Philip had ended the call suddenly. He put down his phone as Paula and Monica replaced theirs. He shrugged as he opened the door, ready to dash down the stairs to his car with Paula at his heels. As Tweed opened the front door she glanced back. Harry had followed them silently down the staircase, was now scuttling out the back way where the transport was kept.

'I wonder what Harry was up to in such a rush?' she mused as she fastened her seat belt.

'Working on some job. You know I give them all latitude to do their own thing.'

'Philip sounded unusually tense,' she remarked as Tweed drove away from Park Crescent, heading towards the motorway which would take them south. 'Maybe we should bother about this Doubenkian,' she suggested.

'Oh, I don't think so,' he said dismissively.

'Well I think we should bother,' she persisted. 'Philip knows what he's talking about. Always.'

'Belt up,' Tweed said cheerfully. 'We're going to have an uneventful day in the country in this lovely spring weather. Relax.'

'Said he was dangerous,' Paula went on.

Tweed looked at her, smiled. He didn't make any further comment, settled down behind the wheel to enjoy a peaceful day.

1

They were driving deep into the countryside, having left the motorway ages ago. The sun still shone out of a clear sea-blue sky. They had met no traffic for a long stretch. Nor were there any more isolated houses with front gardens blooming with spring flowers. Paula's mobile buzzed. She had a short conversation.

'That was Monica,' she said as she pocketed it.

'Really?' said Tweed as though his thoughts were miles away.

'Monica traced where Philip called from. Somewhere in Belgium. Don't know where. They'd only give Monica the country. I didn't think that was one of Philip's happy hunting areas.'

'It isn't normally. But he roams round the Continent.'

'Have you noticed the light aircraft that has been flying roughly on a parallel course to this road?'

'Yes. I have noticed.'

'Maybe it's Marler watching over us.'

'No. Not his aircraft.'

'It's flashing a light now, on and off. What's it doing?'

'No idea.'

'It's stopped. It's flying away north now.'

'So it is.'

She glanced at Tweed. He was answering automatically, as though his mind was elsewhere. He had slowed down as they approached the crest of a high hill, was almost crawling. From the crest they had a panoramic view of the countryside ahead before the lane sloped downwards to a long straight stretch. No more than half a mile ahead, a huge tractor was perched on top of a small hill. The field behind it was ploughed. Large chunks of soil paraded back as far as the eye could see. Tweed stopped, turned off his engine. In the sudden silence the only noise was a faint whine. The digger was stopped but the driver, a vague motionless figure, had kept his motor running. Tweed started his own engine, began moving slowly down the hill. Paula had expected speed. Checking the speedometer she saw they were crawling at a maximum of 25 m.p.h.

Puzzled, she glanced at Tweed. She had never seen him look more relaxed. She was itching to press her foot on the accelerator.

'You could move faster along this stretch,' she suggested. 'We can see miles ahead. Nothing coming the other way.'

'You're right,' he agreed quietly.

They began moving at forty towards the bottom of the hill. Paula sank back in her seat. This was the life. She had her window down and the freshest air in the world filled her nostrils.

They reached the bottom of the hill and Tweed slowed to thirty. Paula glanced at him. He was in a strange mood, but he was probably turning over in his mind aspects of his visit to Bella Main's HQ.

'I'm looking forward to seeing what Hengistbury Manor is like . . .' she began.

'You have got your seat belt fixed properly?' he asked with an edge to his voice.

'Of course I have. Ever since we left Park Crescent.'

'Then sit up straight. And don't chatter. I want to concentrate.'

'All right.' She was peeved. 'I'll be as quiet as a church mouse.'

'Do that.'

They were now moving at forty. Tweed suddenly dropped to thirty again. Then down to twenty-five. He braked suddenly. Paula saw the giant digger just ahead, almost above them, its fearsome caterpillars grinding down through a gap in the hedge. It was making the devil of a noise as it crashed down onto the road.

For a second the massive left-hand caterpillar track, revolving like a terrible mincing machine, filled the windscreen. It passed within inches of their front bumper. Paula was terrified. Tweed sat very still.

The digger's momentum carried it forward across the road as it headed into a gap in the hedge on the other side of the road, out of control. Paula had a glimpse of the driver, wearing a cloth cap and workman's clothes. Panicking, he was desperately trying to find the brake lever, wobbling about inside the cab. Beyond the gap was a smooth slope on the right-hand side, just wide enough for the digger to ascend it to safety.

But to the left of the smooth slope half the gap fell sheer into a rocky gorge. Still panicking, the driver lost control. As the machine mounted the slope the left-hand caterpillar slid over the edge. The whole machine toppled over sideways, plunging into the gorge at speed. Paula had a grisly glimpse of the cab with its driver falling upside down and heard the hideous sound of crushing metal.

The driver had managed to jerk open a window, his head and shoulders projecting. The immense weight of the machine thundered down onto his skull, crushing it to less than half its normal size. Paula let out her breath. Tweed gazed at the carnage for only a brief moment, then drove on down the lane.

'Shouldn't we check on him?' whispered Paula.

'No point. Dead as a dodo. Which was how we were supposed to end up.'

'Maybe we should report it to the police,' she suggested.

'We should *not*! We were supposed to end up inside this car, our bodies flattened like pancakes. Getting involved with the police would cause hours of delay, explanation we don't want to give.'

'Why?' she asked, her voice stronger.

'Obviously someone doesn't want us to reach Hengistbury Manor. It was well planned by a good organizer.'

Paula sensed Tweed didn't wish to pursue this notion. Tactfully she changed the subject.

'Hengistbury is a strange name.'

'Comes from hundreds of years ago. The Jutes – from Jutland – had landed on the Isle of Thanet. Under the command of Hengist and Horsa. They destroyed the Picts who were swarming south to kill the locals. They moved off Thanet and took over large sections of fertile land. It was the beginning of the establishment of the English race. Whoever founded the manor had a sense of history.'

They had reached the top of another hill. Tweed paused. Below the landscape changed dramatically. Instead of rolling open fields they were looking down on an endless sweep of dark green trees as far as the eye could see. Huge tall firs were so close together they looked like an immense cushion, branches often intermingling. Paula almost gasped.

'This must be The Forest, marked on my map. Seems to go on forever.'

'And somewhere inside there is the mansion.'

'Well, I've guided you on the right track.'

As they reached the bottom of the hill she indicated an ancient signpost pointing the way they were headed. *Hengistbury*. The sun, still blazing down, vanished. They were now driving through a dark tunnel, hemmed in overhead and on both sides by stands of firs with massive trunks. Tweed had put on his head-lights full beam. Soon a massive ten-foot-high stone wall appeared on their left, continued for a long dis-tance. It was topped by rolls of barbed wire.

'Have we reached Mrs Bella Main's property?' Paula wondered.

'I think so. She must have scores of acres . . .'

He had just spoken when his headlights illuminated closed wrought-iron gates breaking into the sky-high wall. Tweed glanced in his rear-view mirror, slowed, stopped. Paula glanced back, frowned.

'That car has been following us for a while. I saw it earlier.'

'It's Harry. He's pulled up behind us. Here he comes.'

This had happened before when either Tweed or Paula drove off on their own or together. A member of his dedicated staff would quietly follow them. Prior to the digger incident there had been other attempts in previous cases to kill Tweed. Tweed lowered his window as the Cockney arrived on foot.

'Lost you for a short while on the motorway,' Harry remarked. 'Got stuck in a traffic jam. Then caught on you'd taken the side road south-west. I—'

'Harry,' Tweed ordered, 'don't be seen. Creep up to those gates, see if there's a drive leading straight to the manor. Also check that track on the right opposite the gates. I'll want you to park your car out of sight but so you can see the manor if possible.'

Harry was off at a run, keeping close to the wall. He dropped to his knees, crawled a few paces, peered. He jerked his head to the right to glance at the track. Then he was racing back to the cars.

'What are you up to now?' Paula wondered.

'Wait.' Tweed turned to Harry, back at his window. The Cockney was grinning.

'Piece of cake. Drive runs straight to Buckingham Palace. I'll take the car into the undergrowth here, come round onto that track from behind. What's the game?'

'I'm hoping I'll be near a window so I can signal you by flashing my lighter. That is if anyone leaves the manor by car while we're inside. If so, follow them discreetly.'

'I'm always discreet. Have fun . . . Oh, there's a speakerphone in the nearest pillar. Let's hope they think you're respectable enough to let in!'

Tweed was on the move as Harry's car disappeared into a wilderness of undergrowth. Paula shivered. With

13

the canopy of firs overhead it was chilly. Arriving opposite the tall gates, Tweed swung the car round ready for entrance.

'Wow!' exclaimed Paula. 'I see why he said Buckingham Palace.'

A wide straight drive of small pebbles led straight across parkland for a couple of hundred yards to the manor. The HQ of the Main Chance Bank was an ancient and enormous house obviously built in Elizabethan times. Twirly chimneys reared up everywhere from the roof. At each end of the immense span of the manor projected small extensions, the roofs again supporting more palisades of corkscrew-shaped chimneys. Smoke coiled up from many of them into the windless sky.

Tweed had opened his door to get out and approach the speakerphone when a man's cut-glass voice exploded from the instrument.

'Mr Tweed, Miss Grey, welcome to Hengistbury.'

The gates were already swinging open inwards. Slowly Tweed drove forward. In his rear-view mirror he saw them already closing behind him.

'Must be the finest example of Elizabethan architecture in England,' he commented.

'Fabulous,' Paula almost gasped. 'And so is the park.'

On either side of the drive stretched trim green lawn. On their left a tall fountain jetted high into the air, forming the letter 'H'. To their right the lawn was narrower, and beyond it The Forest's giant firs closed in as though ready to swallow up the park. Paula found them sinister.

'Nothing disturbing, I'm sure,' Tweed remarked.

'Don't be too sure,' Paula responded in a quiet voice.

POCKET
BOOKS

Rhinoceros
COLIN FORBES

"NO ONE IS WHAT THEY SEEM TO BE . . ."

Who is Lisa Trent, mysterious redhead who warns
Tweed of impending catastrophe? Aides to top
statesmen in Washington, London, Paris, Berlin are
murdered by the invisible Mr Blue.

Tweed, Paula and Newman race to East Sussex to
view the second victim, then back to London
which, mercifully, they reach alive. Tweed meets
slippery Gavin Thunder, flamboyant Oskar Vernon,
the devious Mrs France, murderous Delgado. Lisa –
fleeing for her life – keeps reappearing.

Pursuing the secret Elite Club, Tweed and his team
fly to Hamburg, meet a key informant – just before
he too is murdered. The frenetic pursuit leads to
ancient Flensburg on the Danish border, the team
always under attack.

But who is Rhinoceros? Could it be urbane Victor
Rondel, partner in the world's richest bank? The
startling climax erupts violently on Berg island in
the Baltic.

ISBN 978-0-7434-1522-4
£6.99

POCKET
BOOKS

The Vorpal Blade
COLIN FORBES

An investigation into a number of horrific and apparently disconnected murders sweeps Tweed across the world.

The Vorpal Blade advances into gripping new territory. Tweed has reverted to his one-time role of Homicide Superintendent at the Yard. He also retains his position as Deputy Director of the SIS. Paula Grey and Bob Newman still assist him.

Tweed has suspicions about the strange Arbogast banking family. Roman, the bank's owner; his niece, the brilliant Marienetta; his daughter, the volatile Sophie. Wherever they go, the American Vice President follows. Why?

Tweed realizes enormous power lies behind the five murders. But it is shrewd, stubborn Paula Grey, risking her life, who eventually tracks down the wielder of the blade. By herself, underground in a remote mountainous zone.

ISBN 978-0-7434-4035-6
£6.99

POCKET
BOOKS

The Cell
COLIN FORBES

Is Al-Qa'eda about to attack London? Tweed,
reverting to his one-time role as shrewd detective, is
convinced of this. Aided by Paula Grey and Bob
Newman, he skilfully eludes Government security
services who believe that he is wrong.

The village of Carpford, hidden high in the North
Downs, catches Tweed's attention. With its strange
assortment of inhabitants – Victor Warner, arrogant
Minister of Security; fascinating but duplicitous Eva
Brand; Margesson, fanatical preacher – could it be a
staging post for terrorists? Key informants start to
disappear overnight.

Time has run out. This Tweed does know. But what
is the target and when will the attack be launched?
And where?

Will it happen? As it did in America?

ISBN 978-0-7434-6138-2
£6.99

POCKET
BOOKS

No Mercy
COLIN FORBES

A man is found by Chief Superintendent
Buchanan sitting on the steps of Whitehall. The
man has apparently lost his memory. He utters
only three words: *I witnessed murder* ... Buchanan
calls him Michael, hands him over to a reluctant
Tweed, ex-Scotland Yard star detective, now
Deputy Director of the SIS. Events lead Tweed
with his assistant, Paula Grey, to desolate
Dartmoor, accompanied by Michael. There they
discover two skeletons. Later, two more – one in
London, the fourth on a Sussex canal boat.

The wealthy Volkanian family, from Armenia, have a
mansion on Dartmoor. Are they involved? Key
characters are Lucinda Voyles and Anne Barton. There
is a new development. A strange freighter, cargo holds
empty, is spotted heading from the Mediterranean
towards the Cornish coast. Tweed suspects the vessel
is linked to the four horrific murders.

The relentless pace of Tweed's investigation
accelerates. Can he break the case before a sinister
deadline? He fights ruthlessly to do so – in a
riveting double climax.

ISBN 978-0-7434-9001-6
£6.99

POCKET
BOOKS

Blood Storm
COLIN FORBES

Three brothers, known as The Cabal, plot to convert Britain into Police State GB. Tweed and Paula of the SIS are battling to stop the merger of SIS, MI5, the police, the Coastguards, into one massive unit – the sinister State Security. The Cabal has convinced nearly half the Cabinet.

Then Tweed is asked by Commander Buchanan to investigate the horrific murder of society beauty, Viola Vander-Browne. As he struggles to identify the murderer, he is faced with the horrific murder of Viola's twin sister, the raunchy Marina.

Once ace detective at Scotland Yard, Tweed tracks the killer with one hand. With the other he ruthlessly opposes the formation of State Security. Tweed has, from early on, insisted there is a link between the murders and the creation of State Security.

Will the third victim be saved in time? Will State Security be crushed? The desperate pace continues to the explosive climax . . .

ISBN 978-0-7434-9584-4
£6.99

THE MAIN CHANCE
COLIN FORBES

Bella Main, regal owner of the Main Chance, the world's largest private bank, invites her friend Tweed to visit her at Hengistbury Manor, the bank's HQ. Located in a massive Elizabethan mansion, hidden away in The Forest, in the deep south of Britain, the atmosphere is eerie and oppressive.

Bella tells Tweed and Paula that the ruthless European banker, Dubenkian, originally from east of Armenia, has demanded she sells him her bank. She has refused his offer. One week later Bella is horrifically murdered.

Tweed returns with Paula, determined to track the killer. All chief executives of the bank are members of the Main or Chance family. Tweed has already detected hate and deceit among the families. The prison-like effect of working in isolation has created a dangerous sense of hostility. There are more murders. Who is to blame?

There is a devastating surprise when Tweed proves the bank, founded in 1912, was created by a brutal crime all those years ago.

ISBN 978-1-4165-1123-6
£6.99

POCKET
BOOKS

This book and other **Colin Forbes** titles are
available from your local bookshop or can be ordered
direct from the publisher.

978-0-7434-1522-4	Rhinoceros	£6.99
978-0-7434-4035-6	The Vorpal Blade	£6.99
978-0-7434-6138-2	The Cell	£6.99
978-0-7434-9001-6	No Mercy	£6.99
978-0-7434-9584-4	Blood Storm	£6.99
978-1-4165-1123-6	The Main Chance	£6.99
978-1-4165-2643-8	The Savage Gorge	£6.99

Please send cheque or postal order for the value of the book,
free postage and packing within the UK, to
SIMON & SCHUSTER CASH SALES
PO Box 29, Douglas Isle of Man, IM99 1BQ
Tel: 01624 677237, Fax: 01624 670923
Email: bookshop@enterprise.net
www.bookpost.co.uk

Please allow 14 days for delivery. Prices and availability
subject to change without notice